MEDLEY

CHANGING LANES #2

LAYLA REYNE

ABOUT
MEDLEY

Sebastian Stewart was never Mr. Dependable; he was more the good-time guy who only wanted to swim, party, and ink tattoos. Until he cost his team the Olympic gold four years ago. Bas is determined to do right this time around—by his medley relay team and his rookie mentee.

Jacob Burrows is in over his head. The Olympic experience—from the hazing, to the endless practices, to the unrelenting media—makes the shy nineteen-year-old's head spin. He's trying to be everything to everyone while trying not to fall for his gorgeous tattooed teammate who just gets him—gets his need to fix things, his dorky pirate quips, and his bisexuality.

When Jacob falters under the stress, threatening his individual races and the medley relay gold, he needs Bas's help to escape from drowning. Bas, however, fearing a repeat of his mistakes four years ago, pushes Jacob away, sure he'll only let Jacob down. But the only path to salvaging gold is for Jacob to finally ask for what he needs—the heart of the man he loves—and for Bas to become the dependable one.

For me.

CHAPTER
ONE

Lawyer, priest, shrink.

Maybe bartender.

Ask someone to name their confessor and those were the usual suspects.

Bas would argue tattoo artist for the last spot in the top five. Humming needle in hand, he'd heard more than a few confessions over the years.

From the second a client stepped into his shop, they told a story. The design they picked. How much liquid courage it took. The tale of joy or woe that spilled from their lips after the first shock of the needle. Their reaction when it was done—relief, pain, regret, pleasure.

He'd heard almost every story.

In love, in lust, in rebellion, in hate, in freedom, in chains.

But he still couldn't figure out the story that'd nagged him most the past ten days. He swiveled on the stool in the rented studio, droplets of dark ink splattering his worn jeans. "You gonna give me something to go on, Pup?"

Straddling the fancy tattoo-massage chair, Jacob laid a

cheek in the cradle and glanced to his side. Mint green eyes, tequila-hazy, peered out from under long burnished lashes. "This was your idea, not mine."

Maybe there was the start of a story. Why did his nineteen-year-old teammate have a fake ID, and why was he so friendly with Mr. Cuervo? Was it the same story as countless other college undergraduates?

Bas didn't think so.

Jacob's eyes slipped shut again, lips turning up in a faint smile. "You said you needed to get out of there and work." He shrugged his bare left shoulder, the one closest to Bas. The breaststroker's upper back was wide, like most swimmers', his delts and lats hard and lean beneath suntanned skin. Not yet fully developed, given his age, but stronger than most. "So do what you need," Jacob said. "Work it out."

There.

There was the start of the story.

In the week and a half of intensive training since qualifying for the US Olympic Team and being selected for the medley relay squad, Jacob Burrows had been what everyone else needed him to be. The sense of humor Bas's too-tense best friend and team captain, Alex, needed. The single swimmer willing to suffer poster boy and team pariah, Dane. A blank canvas for Bas to work on after a crazy Media Day when the simmering tension between Alex and Dane had boiled over, and Dane had leapt off his ivory pedestal.

Whatever anyone else needed.

But who was Jacob? A steadily improving swimmer at the

University of Texas, the rising junior had gotten his first big win at Trials, shattering the two-hundred-meter breaststroke US record. One hell of an entrance onto the elite competitive swimming scene, and one hell of a fire to be thrown into. Now he was the youngest rookie, "the pup," on a USA Swimming team riddled with drama, even more so than the drama Bas had caused four years ago. And they weren't even in Madrid yet. Jacob deftly juggled the team dynamics, but surely the pressure was mounting on him too. What did *he* need? And why did Jacob put everyone else's needs before his own? Pure altruism or something more? Or less?

And right here, right now, was *Bas* taking advantage of those selfless tendencies? He should stop. Tell the shop-cat out front that the pup had changed his mind. Happened all the time at Bas's tattoo shop back in LA. He was sure it'd be nothing new here in San Antonio either. Or maybe Jacob did need this. Maybe needle to skin would loosen his tongue enough to tell Bas his story.

What Jacob needed.

Alex had asked Bas to watch over the rook while they kept their secret weapon hidden from the media and other teams. To do that, Bas needed to know what he was dealing with—when and where the cracks might appear—so he could help Jacob. It was no less than Jacob's selflessness deserved, and the least Bas could do, after being so selfish on his last Olympic tour. If tonight was his chance to help Jacob and his team, then he'd make the most of the offered opportunity, the way he knew best. Through his art.

Closing his eyes, Bas bounced his fist on his knee as he

visualized the design. Something Jacob wouldn't regret when the tequila wore off. Something he'd later look at with pride and others would look at in awe. Something for the Texas Longhorn who was training for his first Olympics in his home state. The artwork came together in Bas's mind: long curved lines woven to create horns; sharp lines angled in an inverse triangle to form a snout; touches of burnt orange at the ends of each nostril and where its eyes should be. Given creative license, he had no problem inking this freehand.

At the first touch of the needle on the outside of his shoulder, Jacob gasped. Eyes scrunched closed, crooked front teeth digging into his full lower lip, Jacob clawed at the padded bar beneath the face cradle.

"Breathe through it." Bas laid his right hand on Jacob's lower back, giving his subject's senses a different focal point. Jacob's breathing hitched, then began to steady, the visibly pounding pulse in his neck slowing as well. Bas gave him another few seconds, another few measured breaths, inhaling and exhaling with him, before he began drilling again.

"Why do you do that?" Bas asked.

"Do what?" Jacob said, voice cracking adorably.

"Put everyone else first."

Jacob moved to shrug, and Bas raised the needle in the nick of time. "Don't do that," he chided, drumming warning taps on Jacob's spine. "Unless you want a mess here."

"Sorry, sorry," Jacob said, half-smiling, half-grimacing. He resettled his temple in the cradle, face angled toward Bas. "Why'd you start tattooing?"

"Don't do that either."

"What? I want to be sure the guy inking me knows what he's doing."

Bas gestured at his own arms and shoulders, covered with colorful artwork. He'd ditched his shirt earlier, the shop's AC no match for the triple-digit heat.

"You didn't do all those tats yourself," Jacob said.

"No, but I designed them all."

Jacob's lingering gaze across his chest and arms left a different sort of heat in its wake, warmth that rippled down Bas's neck and back as he bent his head and continued to work. He'd caught enough of Jacob's appreciative looks to suspect the pup was bisexual like him, if not gay like Alex. But Bas hadn't acted on those looks—no drama. Teammates—other athletes, for that matter—were strictly off-limits. Regardless of how charming their green eyes, crooked teeth, and pirate quips might be.

"What's the most personal?" Jacob asked. "They all look like team tats or abstract designs, except the initials on your chest. Who's JE?"

Speaking of drama, or rather not speaking of it . . . "It's not usually the artist who tells his story."

"But isn't that what art is?"

"This art's about you." Bas drummed his fingers over Jacob's spine again, and Jacob hummed contentedly, eyes drifting closed on another lazy smile.

"What are you drawing about me?" Jacob asked after a few minutes.

"You'll have to wait and see. Now, answer my question."

"I've forgotten it."

Bas chuckled. "Bullshit."

"I put myself first once. It didn't end well."

Bas's laughter died and his insides knotted, hearing Jacob's words and seeing how fast his toothy smile had fled. Another page of his story: not a happy one. But before Bas could read further, before he could ask who'd burned this too-gentle soul, and how Bas could avenge him, Jacob closed the book.

"I'm only nineteen," he said, voice bright again, albeit falsely so. "I learn more watching and looking out for others."

Bas flattened his hand on the pup's warm, muscled back. "But who's looking out for you, Jacob?"

JACOB.

Not *kid*.

Not *Pup*.

Jacob.

Bas had called him by his name, together with a gentle hand on his back and a soft question that had sounded more like a promise.

"But who's looking out for you, Jacob?"

As good as a carrot dangled in front of a starving rabbit. A carrot that came with a two-letter caveat—*JE*—whoever the hell that was. Jacob was still starving, regardless.

From the first touch of the needle, he'd been hard.

No, that was a lie.

He'd been hard since Bas had stripped off his shirt and sat on the stool next to him in just his jeans, but Jacob was trying to ignore all that.

The blond dreadlocks piled atop of his teammate's head. The striking blue eyes and laser-cut cheekbones. The tattoos decorating his fly-swimmer's massive upper body. The powerful thighs Jacob had dreamed about straddling him every night since meeting Sebastian Stewart at Trials.

Failing to ignore, clearly.

Thankfully, before he embarrassed himself by coming in his pants or babbling a too-telling answer to Bas's question, his teammate's phone rang. Queen's thumping "Under Pressure" was enough to snap the tension.

Bas switched off the tattoo machine. "That's Alex. Let me take this."

"Yeah, go," Jacob said, chuckling at the too-perfect song choice.

Bas stood and stepped into the far corner, phone to his ear, while Jacob adjusted himself in the chair, breathing a sigh of relief on multiple fronts. They'd both been worried after this afternoon's press conference—Bas for his best friend, Jacob for Alex *and* Dane, and also for himself. Coach had warned them that Media Day would be intense, but Jacob had had no idea it would be *that* bonkers. The endless clicking of cameras, reporters doggedly shouting questions, sponsors eyeing their next paychecks, and all that was before Dane had dropped an innocuous comment that'd exploded like a cluster bomb. So much attention, at domestic training.

What would greet them in Vienna at their international training site, or in Madrid once they finally reached the Olympics?

After the presser, questions and dread had swirled in Jacob's head, keeping pace with Bas's circuits around their shared hotel room. Not even the bottle of tequila they'd nursed together had calmed them down. So when Jacob had asked what Bas needed, and Bas had answered, "To get out and work," Jacob had happily obliged, for both their sakes. They'd ended up here—in a stuffy tattoo parlor down the street from Jacob's old high school.

Bas glanced across the room at him, grinning as he rolled his eyes, probably at something Alex said. When he strode back over after another minute, his relief was palpable, his big body relaxed. "All good. He's got Big Red." Bas straddled the stool and picked up the tattoo machine again, flipping it on. "Told them to stay out for a bit."

"Probably a good idea." Jacob squirmed in the chair, resituating himself and girding his loins against the bite of the needle and the nearness of Bas. Not wanting to destroy the calm with more of his sad story, Jacob asked about swimming instead—the team, their competition, what to expect at the Olympics—and Bas let him have that dodge. Returning the favor, Jacob didn't press when Bas skirted questions about his particular experience four years ago. The loss of the medley relay gold hung heavy over the team; a weight that grew heavier each day the closer they got to Madrid.

Tonight, though, the weight in Jacob's balls was a bigger

problem. The youngest on the team, surrounded by professionals, and swimming medley relay with Bas, Alex, and Dane, who were all in their midtwenties and members of high-profile clubs, Jacob had tried, over the past two weeks and today, to act more mature. His hormones, however, didn't give a flying fuck about his intentions.

The next hour was pure torture, with Jacob's lower lip bearing the brunt of it. The worst came at the end, when Bas held up his phone with the camera inverted and showed Jacob the tattoo he'd inked onto Jacob's outer left shoulder.

An intricately styled Longhorn. Perfect for him. And as gorgeous as the artist.

Jacob blinked back the moisture in his eyes and bit his tongue against saying more than "It's awesome."

Bas arched a blond brow as he dabbed on salve. "Just 'awesome'?"

Jacob smiled through the strain, hoping like hell it didn't look too lopsided, confused as his body was right then. "Fucking awesome."

Bas smiled wide, and Jacob barely contained his moan. As soon as Bas stood, Jacob tumbled out of the chair, miraculously managing not to land on his face, and darted into the changing room.

His shoulder was on fire, but the blazing sting there was nothing compared to the scorching heat that had burned through him the entire time he'd sat in that chair. Heat that needed a release. Glancing over his shoulder, through the narrow slit in the dressing room curtains, Jacob spotted Bas way up front, chatting with the shop girl. Far enough away and suitably distracted. Jacob decided to risk it. He had to, unless he was going to walk out of here with a boner the size of Texas. He didn't want to risk *that*; he was embarrassed enough already.

He moved away from the curtain's gap and closer to the wall, unzipping his jeans as he thought about the shop girl. Her dark curls and warm brown eyes, her full lips painted cherry red, her matching push-up bra teasing the collar of her low-cut tank, tits spilling out over the lacy cups. Reaching a hand inside his boxers, he stroked his aching dick and bit back a groan, imagining the girl's lips around his cock and the view of her overflowing breasts from above. Lost in the fantasy, he fell back against the wall, landing on his tender tattoo, and blinding pain erased the vision. Gritting his teeth to keep from shouting out, he spun to face the wall, left hand braced next to the mirror, right hand back down his pants.

He closed his eyes and brought the girl to mind again. Her bright red lips, her tits in matching lace, the colorful tattoo sleeves decorating her arms. But then her willowy arms grew bigger, more muscular, and they were covered in coarse blond hair and familiar colorful designs. Her cherry red lips faded to pale pink, surrounded by rough dark blond stubble, and her brown eyes morphed to piercing blue. Jacob's cock swelled in his hand, leaking moisture and slicking his fumbling grip. He yanked it out of his jeans and boxers and jerked faster. Head bowed, he imagined another cock sliding against his own, held tightly in his grasp. Or in the grasp of—

"Hey, Pup, how long's it take to put your shirt back on?"

The dressing room curtain swung open, and Jacob, dick in hand, stared at the blue eyes of his fantasy in the mirror. "Fuck!" He quickly cast his gaze aside, struggling to stuff his interested, uncooperative dick back in his boxers. "Sorry, sorry."

"You're not the first, Pup." Jacob's eyes shot back to the mirror. Bas was smiling, wicked and teasing. "You're not even in the double digits."

Double digits of what? To jerk off after getting a tattoo? Or to jerk off to him? Or in front of him?

Fuck, that thought would not go away.

"It's not an uncommon reaction after getting a tattoo," Bas clarified. "The rush, the endorphins, the response some people have to pain."

Jacob had personally never associated the two—pleasure and pain. Then again, he'd never had them delivered together before, much less by someone so attractive.

"Do what you need," Bas said, taking a step back and moving to draw the curtain closed again.

Do what you need.

Which was what? The answer was out, spoken, the moment Jacob thought it. "Stay."

Bas froze, hand fisting the thick velvet curtain. "Jacob."

Grip tightening at his name in Bas's rough, rumbling voice, Jacob closed his eyes, craving the fantasy for real. He shouldn't ask. It was too much, more than Bas had offered. He asked too much and people left. But maybe he could ask for less than the entire fantasy, just enough of what he needed. "You don't have to do anything. I just don't . . ." God, how did he ask this and not sound like a loser?

The curtain rattled closed, and Jacob's heart sank, sure Bas had left. But it rocketed into his throat when, a second later, Bas, in his deep voice, asked, "What do you need, Jacob?"

"I don't want to be alone."

Bas's hand fell gently on his back, a shot of warmth right where it'd concentrated earlier as he'd sat in the chair. "I'm here," Bas said.

Heat purled, arrowing in a direct line from Bas's hand to Jacob's dick. Jacob wrangled himself free of his boxers and resumed pumping, harder and faster, so close to the edge as the fantasy revived behind his eyelids.

And spiraled.

Bas's powerful thighs driving against his. His big wide chest blanketing Jacob's back. Cheek to cheek, blond dreadlocks falling loose around their faces. Bas's cock in his ass, where no one else had been before, and his calloused hand around Jacob's dick, fingers entwined, jerking him off together.

"Let go," Bas commanded softly.

Jacob came, a whimpered "Sebastian" tumbling from his lips.

CHAPTER
TWO

Nine.

That was how many times Jacob had started and discarded whatever he was writing at the desk, only to try again after a lap around their room and some piecemeal packing. It'd been two hours since they'd left Alex and Dane's room, and while Bas had finished one sketch and started another, the pup had little to show for all his nervous energy. Not that Bas hadn't been as bad last week after the gonzo press conference, waiting for Alex's call.

Propped against the headboard, Bas tracked a tenth ball of crumpled paper as it whizzed past, missing the trash can by a mile. The pup's aim was as bad as his hair, even if they both made Bas smile. It'd been a week since Media Day, the night before which Bas had fixed Jacob's half-shaven head, buzzing the entire thing. Now, fuzzy blond hair was growing back, unevenly, making Jacob look like a Chia Pet in progress.

Bas tossed his graphics tablet aside and swung his legs off the bed. "All right, Pup, let's go."

Jacob froze mid-lap. "Go where?"

Bas grabbed the electric clippers off the table between their beds. "Bathroom," he said. "We need to fix your hair before we leave."

"But we're flying out of Houston. No press there."

"I'll believe that when I see it." Bas nudged him toward the bathroom. "And regardless, I'm not letting you go out in public like that."

Jacob glared over his shoulder, almost running into a wall. "You let me go out in public last night, to the food trucks with Dane and Alex."

"After I told you to put on that raggedy-ass UT baseball cap."

"Some mate you are." Plopping down on the toilet, Jacob shrugged out of his T-shirt part way, one long arm getting caught in the collar. "Arrrgh!"

Laughing, Bas helped him the rest of the way out of the shirt, coaching himself not to linger on his teammate's tan skin and lean muscles. This was like any other day on deck or in the locker room; it wasn't like that night a week ago in the cozy tattoo parlor. He shouldn't have indulged himself then, but Jacob wrecked with lust—pupils blown wide, skin flushed, erect cock in hand, and the dimples at the base of his spine calling Bas's name—had been beyond beautiful, like a work of art Bas couldn't turn away from. And when Jacob had begged him to stay, it'd tugged like a magnet at Bas's insides. The same way the pup's pirate quips, goofy hair, and refusal to admit what had him tied in nervous knots drew Bas to him tonight.

After plugging in the clippers, Bas flipped them on, and

their low, steady buzz filled the room. He skated the clippers over Jacob's scalp, hand trailing to brush away loose hairs and lift any stragglers. Jacob shivered on the first pass, tension tightening his spine and shoulders, but as Bas continued the repetitive motions, Jacob's spine and shoulders curled forward, his entire body swaying with each pass of the blades.

When he was good and relaxed, all the nervous energy wrung out of him, Bas began to dig, carefully. "You wanna tell me what's got you worked up?"

"Worked up?" Jacob mumbled, half in a daze.

"You lapped the room nine times and made a mess of your luggage in the process. All two bags of it."

Jacob's swaying stopped, as did his responses.

Bas tried another avenue. "What were you writing?"

"Notes," he answered, defiant green eyes flickering up at Bas.

Bas pressed anyway. "You were fine when we were in Alex and Dane's room."

"Too busy stuffing my face with BBQ." After a moment, he added quietly, as if to speak the words would risk them coming true, "What if the Committee doesn't reinstate him?"

Earlier that day, Alex and Dane had returned to San Antonio with evidence that Alex had been framed by another teammate for doping. A lawyer's kid, Bas thought the exculpatory evidence looked pretty damn convincing—Coach Hartl had agreed—but ultimately the US Olympic Committee would make the call. Hopefully they'd make it before the team was scheduled to fly out of tomorrow. Bas wanted his best friend and captain on that flight with them, but he had to be prepared for the worst-case scenario. And Jacob should be too.

"If he's not reinstated," Bas said, the words leaving a bad taste in his mouth, "then someone else will swim in his place." The aftertaste was worse.

"But Ryan was Alex's backup," Jacob countered.

Ryan, their individual medley champ and Alex's backstroke and medley relay backup, had been the one who'd framed Alex, angling for his spot in both events.

"Coach will sub in other swimmers, like he did in practice today."

"And the medley relay?" Jacob's voice pitched higher, his shoulders tight again. "We sucked without him in practice today."

"We've got a week until Madrid," Bas said, reassuring himself as much as Jacob. "We'll make it work."

"What if we can't? What if the subs aren't the problem?"

Confused, Bas turned off the clippers and set them aside. "What other problem is there?"

"Me."

For as soft as Jacob's voice actually was, it rang as loud as the starting horn at a meet to Bas, slamming into him and kicking his instincts into action. At a meet, he'd launch off the block into the pool. Here, in this tiny hotel bathroom, he dropped to his knees in front of Jacob. "Is that what's got you nervous?"

Chin tucked, Jacob angled his face away, gnawing at his

lower lip. "I haven't been doing this as long as you guys."

"Doesn't mean you're not the best." Cautiously, as he'd seen Jacob do before, Bas laid his hands on Jacob's knees and waited for Jacob to give him his eyes again. "You have a new national record to show for it."

Jacob lifted a hand, a single finger raised. "From one race." He lowered the digit and flitted the raised hand between them. "The races before that . . ."

"What about them?"

He dropped his hand onto his thigh, just out of Bas's reach. "I couldn't pull out the win. I choked."

Bas slid his hand forward, covering Jacob's. "Or you didn't know how to win yet. You've won now. You just have to keep winning."

"I don't know how."

His small, anxious voice tugged again at Bas's insides. So did the question Jacob wouldn't ask; Bas heard it all the same. "We'll show you how."

Jacob's answering smile was wobbly and tired. Bas could continue to push this, or he could let it go and try taking Jacob's mind off his worries. Perhaps he needed that more than a confidence boost tonight.

Bas stood, unplugged the clippers, and wrapped the cord around the handle. "I heard about this supposedly awesome pirate show on TV."

Head falling back, Jacob looked up at him with unconcealed relief. And delight. "*Black Sails?*"

"That's the one." Bas smiled as he stepped back, making room for Jacob to stand. "Was thinking I might check out an episode or two. Decide if I wanted to download more for the flight tomorrow."

"Aye, matey, nothing *supposed* about it. You're definitely going to walk that plank." Smile surer now, Jacob ran a hand over his freshly shorn head and turned toward the shower. "Cue it up while I rinse off."

Wandering back into their room, Bas ignored the running water and images that teased his subconscious. He'd done right by his team and Jacob tonight. If he could just keep doing right the next two weeks, the medley relay gold would be in their grasp.

DOING RIGHT GOT harder the next morning, in more ways than one.

Jacob had fallen asleep next to Bas, in Bas's bed, halfway through the second episode of *Black Sails*. Bas had thought it best to let him sleep rather than risk a return of his earlier nerves. During the night, they'd drifted toward each other, an increasing force of habit, the need to be near each other almost instinctual. Bas knew he should put a stop to it. Christ, even Alex had noticed.

But still Bas indulged.

Like he had in the tattoo parlor a week ago. That night, he'd rationalized his actions as returning the favor, giving Jacob what he needed after the pup had done the same for him. He'd made a similar rationalization last night; he hadn't wanted to wake Jacob.

This morning, though, there was no rationalizing the hour Bas lay awake in bed, holding Jacob tucked against his side, half sprawled across his chest, Jacob's cock digging into his thigh. No rationalizing the near-overwhelming urge to roll over and cover Jacob's inviting mouth and warm body with his own. That was nothing but pure desire, pure want, for the impressive young man Bas was getting to know and like better every day.

But acting on his impulses wouldn't be good for anyone. Not for the team and most of all not for Jacob. History—his own and that of the other men in his family—dictated it wouldn't end well for the pup. Bas had promised Alex he wouldn't fuck things up this time—that he'd look out for the rook—and with Alex's spot on the team in jeopardy, it was even more imperative that Bas keep his promises.

Which was why, when Jacob started to wake and every part of him stiffened—Bas would bet with surprise and embarrassment—Bas closed his eyes and deepened his breathing, feigning sleep. What followed was a serious test of restraint, fighting his desire . . . and laughter.

"Shit!" Jacob cursed low as he scooted out from under Bas's arm and toward the side of the bed. The sheet went sliding with him, then with a muffled "oof" and a thump, the sheet disappeared altogether. Bas peeked through his eyelashes, making sure Jacob wasn't hurt. It was last night's T-shirt incident all over again. Tangled on the floor, Jacob was fighting with the sheet like his life depended on it; how someone with so little control over his limbs was also a world-class swimmer remained a mystery. Bas had to bite his tongue and claw the mattress to keep from shaking with laughter. A string of quiet, sailor-worthy curses later, Jacob finally freed himself, and Bas snapped his eyes closed, still pretending to sleep as Jacob tossed the sheet back over him.

Peeking again after a moment, Bas watched him scurry across the three feet to his bed, tripping over his shoes and tumbling onto the mattress. Jacob smothered a groan in his pillow, and Bas had to roll the other way, toward the wall, to smother a laughing groan of his own.

He was halfway back to sleep when someone knocked on their door. Rolling over, he caught Jacob's confused eyes before they darted away.

"I'll get it," Bas said, climbing out of bed. Down the short hallway, he opened the door to a hassled-looking Coach Hartl.

He held out an airplane ticket envelope, printed with the same logo as the one in Bas's messenger bag. "You want to do the honors?"

Bas flipped it open and read the passenger's name. "Fuck yeah!" he answered, pumping his fist in the air.

"Figured you might." Coach clapped him on the shoulder. "I'm gonna grab a couple hours of sleep before we leave. You fools be on the bus at one."

"Yes, sir." Bas closed the door and fell back against it, smiling wide. "Hey, Pup!" he shouted into the room.

Pink-cheeked, eyes downcast, Jacob appeared around the corner. "What's going on?"

"Throw on some sweats! We've got good news to deliver." He held the ticket aloft. "Captain's back."

Jacob's big green eyes shot up, finally meeting his. "Alex is cleared?"

"Things are looking golden, Pup."

He allowed himself one more indulgence, soaking in the toothy smile that split Jacob's face.

CHAPTER
THREE

Jacob threw his jacket and tie over a kitchen chair and tugged at the collar of his dress shirt, loosening the top button for some relief from the stifling heat. He dug the pad of hotel-branded paper out of his pocket, and tossed it to his cousin. "I've written everything down on there."

He'd finally finished writing out the notes this morning, after they'd given Alex the all-clear news. "I also typed and emailed them to you," he added, acknowledging his own chicken scratch.

Josh rolled his eyes, the same light green shade as Jacob's. "Yeah, cuz, I got 'em." He tossed the notepad on the kitchen counter, then reached out and knuckled Jacob's head. "What the fuck happened to your hair?"

"Now you're complaining? You nagged me all last semester to"—Jacob curled his fingers in air quotes and lowered his voice to match his cousin's deeper register—"cut that fucking mop off."

Josh grinned. "Maybe now you'll get laid."

"Or better yet, I can pretend to be you," Jacob replied, wiping the grin off his cousin's face. "I'll definitely get laid, then."

People already mistook them for brothers. Born on the same day, their fathers brothers, they'd been treated as twins their entire lives, right down to the similar names. Jacob's shaggy hair and Josh's bigger build and deeper voice had been the few things that'd distinguished them. Those and Josh's utter coolness versus Jacob's utter . . . uncoolness. Now, though, with Jacob's hair buzzed and the extra muscle mass he'd put on in Olympic training, they really did look like twins. On the surface at least.

"I like this idea. Mooching off your cred for a while." Jacob loosened another button on his dress shirt, going for cool, on both counts. When that didn't work, on either count, he embraced his inner dork and opened the freezer door, sticking his head inside.

"Fuck this shit," Josh grumbled. "You're going to trash my cred."

Jacob gestured at his buzz cut again. "You asked for it."

"I meant going around sticking your head in freezers, goofball. As for the hair, why'd you do it?"

Jacob pulled his head out of the cold, finally a bit more comfortable. "Easier to deal with. Training, travel, and all that." More like he'd been hazed—one side of his dirty blond curls shaved off the first night of Olympic training in Colorado Springs. He'd played team sports long enough to have expected it, especially since he was the youngest member on the team, but the morning after had been brutal, the altitude in Colorado Springs compounding his margarita-fueled misery. To hear tell it, more hazing awaited him in

Madrid.

Bas had shaved the other half of his head before Media Day, then touched it up again last night, distracting Jacob from what had really been racking his nerves, at least initially. The topic he was trying to have a serious conversion about with his cousin, head in fridge notwithstanding.

He tapped a finger on the notepad. "His doctor's numbers and the clinic's emergency number are all on here and in the email. Plus his list of meds. A couple will need to be refilled before I get back. Make sure he gets them. And I wrote some tips and tricks for calming him, in case he has a flashback."

"Tell him to breathe, remind him it's a flashback, ground him in the present using his senses." Josh clasped the side of Jacob's neck, his hold sure, his bright eyes alert and sympathetic. Under all that swagger, Josh was one of the most dependable, most devoted people Jacob knew. "Chill, cuz. This ain't my first rodeo watching out for your dad while you're at a meet. And Uncle D hasn't had a flashback in two years. Not since we been at UT."

"Austin's an hour and a half away. I could get here, if I needed to."

"And you haven't needed to." He pointed out the kitchen window at the house across the street. "Mom and Dad live right there. I'm home for the summer, right there. I'm the one getting a degree in psychology and working at the VA hospital. We got this."

Head bowed, Jacob scuffed the floor with his dress shoe, staring at the black streak it left on the fading linoleum. "I've never been gone this long."

"Or this far." Josh squeezed his neck, forcing his gaze back up. "I think this is more about you than Uncle Davis." They might not have been brothers, technically, but Josh was his best friend and knew him better than anyone. "How have things been, you know, other than the hair?"

Shaking off Josh's hold, Jacob rested back against the tile counter, fingers curled over the rounded lip. "It's been wild, and it's barely started."

"Yeah, I saw your two teammates on SportsCenter. At the airport . . ."

"Some scene, huh?"

When Dane and Alex had returned yesterday, reporters had been waiting for them at the airport. Dane, the consummate showman, had given them one hell of a spectacle. He'd pledged to clear Alex's name and to stand by the man he loved. Big news for the supposedly straight poster boy son of high-profile conservative parents. Jacob hadn't been all that surprised; the tension between Dane and Alex had been simmering from day one of training.

"It's settled now," he told Josh. "Alex is back on the team, and Dane's, well, Dane." Jacob had sensed there was more beneath Dane's camera-ready smile and had made the effort to remain friendly when others had shunned him. He was glad not to have misjudged the Tar Heel.

"So the guys are being good to you?" Josh asked. "Even with all that shit going on?"

Jacob nodded. "They've taken me under their wing."

Alex regularly checking in with him. Dane helping him

last week when the pressure had all seemed too heavy and the imposter syndrome too real, swimming as he was with giants. Bas shielding him on Media Day, staying with him after. Heat hit his cheeks, remembering that night in the tattoo parlor. They grew even warmer, no doubt redder, with Josh's next question.

"Any of 'em hot?"

"They're my teammates," Jacob said. "That's it."

Yes, he'd jerked off in front of Bas, but after that night a week ago, things had returned to normal. If he ignored how Bas's gaze lingered more often, how he and Bas gravitated toward each other, how he'd fallen asleep next to Bas last night, only to wake with his morning wood pressed against Bas's hard thigh. He'd stumbled over to his own bed before Bas awoke, and thank God it'd been to the excitement of Alex's reinstatement, because Jacob could barely look his mentor in the eyes after his fumbling scurry of shame.

Still failing to ignore, clearly.

"Yeah, I'm gonna have to call bullshit," Josh said. "That ain't a sunburn, cuz, and the teammate thing's not stopping the other two."

Jacob glared at his cousin. "Joshua."

Josh raised his hands, placating even as he smirked. "I know the bi thing's new to you—"

"Bisexuality. And not that new."

Jacob couldn't remember a time he'd thought girls were cuter than boys or vice versa. When puberty and hormones hit, he'd been sexually attracted to men and women. He'd had his first raging crush on a guy four years ago—a certain tattooed butterfly swimmer he'd watched at the Olympics on TV—and his first sexual experience with a guy the summer after high school. He'd been caught blowing one of the lifeguards at the pool where he swam, at which point he'd officially come out to his family.

In the two years since, there'd been Emily from freshman biology, after weeks of working up the nerve to ask her out, and Wes from sophomore anthropology, a handful of dates after months of Jacob's piss-poor flirting. Nothing serious had come of either, owing to his hectic schedule, his aforementioned uncoolness, and his bisexuality. Emily had been paranoid he'd wanted to fuck every guy at UT, while he hadn't been "gay enough" for Wes, whatever the hell that meant. Jacob hadn't been attracted enough to either to outweigh their bullshit, or fret over his virginity. Not like the attraction he felt toward Bas, especially now that he wasn't an out-of-reach swim God. He was real, a friend, and Bas was also bi; he'd get it—get him—like Emily and Wes hadn't. Which only made his enduring virginity more embarrassing, his inexperience, in all regards, more stark.

"Hey, Earth to Jacob." Josh waved a hand in front of his face, snapping Jacob out of his head. "I'm just saying that even my straight self can acknowledge those are some good-looking men on your team. Couldn't blame you for trying to hit a few." Grinning, he slicked a hand over Jacob's head. "Especially now that you're fine like me."

Jacob swatted the hand away. "Yo, Rico Suave, back to reality for a sec."

"Dude," Josh groaned. "You weren't even born when

that song dropped."

"Neither were you." Jacob picked up the notepad again and put it back in his cousin's hand. "My itinerary and all the contact numbers for where we'll be are on the last sheets. And I've turned roaming on for my cell. Call, FaceTime, or Skype if you need me. I don't care what time."

"Like I said, we got this. You don't have to worry." Josh pocketed the notepad and yanked him into a crushing hug. "My boy, at the Olympics."

Jacob broke into a smile, more than a little amazed himself still. Yes, the pressure was a crush, but when he stepped back to look at the big picture, this was what he'd worked so hard for. Long days, countless carpools, and perpetually pruned fingers, but he was going to compete at the Olympics—every kid's dream when they took off between the lane ropes the first time.

"So proud of you, cuz." Pulling back, Josh clapped the outside of his left shoulder, right over the healing tattoo.

Jacob yelped, snatching his arm away.

"You injured?"

Jacob slapped the spot again, fighting the urge to scrape his nails across it instead. "Not an injury." Josh clearly didn't buy his nonanswer one bit, judging by the lift of his bushy blond brow. "Fine," Jacob conceded. "You promise not to tell Dad?"

"Tell him what?"

"I got a tattoo."

Josh's eyes grew round as saucers. "Isn't he gonna see it on TV?"

"Yeah, but by then I'll be an ocean away."

He'd asked to get ink once before, after graduation, when he was still seventeen and needed permission. Instead, he'd gotten a twenty-minute lecture on regret, which Josh had heard all the way across the street. Jacob wouldn't regret this tattoo, but he would regret arguing with his dad before he left. His new ink needed to stay on the DL, for now.

"Fine," Josh said. "I won't tell him. Now let me see it."

"I can't actually show it to you." Jacob pulled out his phone and opened his camera roll. "It's a scabby mess and itches like an army of fire ants gnawing off my arm, so these will have to do." He handed the phone to Josh.

Josh stared down at the screen, jaw slack, as he thumbed through the pictures. "Aww shit, Jacob."

"You don't like it?"

"Are you kidding?" He held the phone closer, spreading his two fingers on the screen and zooming in on the design. "It's fucking badass." He glanced up, eyes big and grin wide. "You might be cooler than me now. Who's the artist and can I get one?"

The front door banged open, forestalling Jacob's answer.

"Did I miss him?" his father shouted from the foyer.

"Nope, still here, Dad." Jacob snatched his phone back and pocketed it just as his father rounded the corner into the kitchen.

"Sorry I'm late." Davis shrugged out of his grease-stained shop shirt, throwing it onto an empty chair. "Knew I had to be home by noon—set an alarm and everything—but I got to working on a '67 Camaro SS. Full engine rebuild."

Josh whistled low.

"You got that right," Davis answered with a smile.

Jacob was happy his dad was back at work and enjoying it. He'd worried the loud garage noises, especially the air compressor that sounded like a machine gun, might trigger his PTSD, but Davis doing what he did best, aside from firing a sniper's rifle, had settled him, for the most part. Asking him to come home, off schedule, was more likely to trigger an anxiety attack than a full day at the garage. Jacob, though, had wanted to say goodbye, in person, before leaving for Europe.

His father seemed all right as he drew Jacob into a hug, careful not to pat directly with his grease-stained hands. "You packed and ready to go?"

"Bags are already on the team bus at the hotel." He checked his watch. "T-minus thirty minutes to departure."

"You got your passport and everything?"

"Cap's got all that stuff."

"Alex looking out for you?" Davis's memory, for better or worse, was sharp as a tack. He never forgot a name.

"Yeah, Dad."

"Good, good." Except he'd started to shift back and forth on his feet and rub his thumb over his left ring finger, where his wedding band no longer rested. "You've never been this far away."

Jacob moved slowly, making sure his dad saw his approaching hand before it landed on top of his and squeezed. "We set our daily call time. I'll ring you each day. It'll be just like when I'm at UT."

His father's smile returned, except it didn't quite reach his eyes. "But you'll be at the Olympics," he said, wonder tangled with worry and sadness. "I'm sorry I can't come with you."

Jacob jutted a thumb at the sixty-inch television on the adjacent living room wall. "You'll have a better view on that thing."

"And I'm gonna stream it," Josh said. "We're gonna watch live and have the whole gang over for the main event."

"I know. I saw the Evite." It comforted Jacob to think of their family and friends gathered here to watch the medley relay race with his dad. He hoped like hell he didn't disappointment them, or the members of his squad.

Davis cleared his throat. "Okay, a couple things to take with you." Face turning bright red, his dad pulled a strip of condoms out of his back jeans pocket and slapped them into Jacob's hand. "You be safe." Three words, and just as awkward as Jacob remembered the same "talk" two years ago.

Jacob's face roasted to match his dad's as he pocketed the strip.

"I hear there are plenty of those around Olympic Village," Josh said.

"Lord, don't tell me that, boy," Davis said. "And you—" he pointed a finger at Jacob "—don't come back and tell me either. I don't wanna know."

Jacob coughed to cover his laugh. "My lips are sealed."

"One more thing." Davis slid his fingers under the chain around his neck and lifted it over his head, his Marine Corps dog tags slipping out from under his shirt collar. Reaching for Jacob's hand, he dropped the body-warmed metal into his palm. "These will keep you safe too."

The lump in Jacob's throat made it hard to talk. "Dad, if you need these . . ." Except for in-patient stints at the clinic, Jacob couldn't recall a time his father had taken the tags off since returning home.

Davis folded his fingers over the tags. "I need to know there's a part of me with you. That I'm still doing my part to keep my boy safe."

His dad had said those same words each time he'd deployed. Doing his part to keep his boy safe.

"Okay, Dad," Jacob replied hoarsely. He pulled his dad into another hug, grease-stains be damned. "Thank you."

"You come back with medals around your neck, and you can give me back those rusty ole things."

Jacob squeezed him tighter. "It's a deal."

THE TEAM BUS parked at the IAH departures curb, and Sean's beleaguered, "Shit, they're here too," echoed from the front of the bus all the way to the back, where Bas had spent the trip from San Antonio.

Tossing his tablet onto the adjacent seat, Bas shifted across the aisle to the empty row behind Alex and Dane to stare out the curbside window. Sure enough, a crowd of waiting press was gathered at the terminal entry.

Alex rammed the heel of his hand against the arm rest. "Fuck! I thought the change in airport would cut this shit out."

Bas poked his head between the two seats in front of him, eyeing his best friend. "And I thought you were smarter than that."

Dane stood and stepped into the aisle, looking perfectly pressed despite the three-hour bus ride. "It'll be fine." He shrugged into his designer sports jacket, adjusted his silk tie, and ran a hand over his thick red-gold hair, taming it down. "I'll just go out there—"

"*I'll* go out there," Coach said, halfway down the aisle to them. "And we're at this airport because it's two less stops to Vienna." He tossed a black pouch into Alex's lap. "Distribute passports and make sure everyone's got their shit. When I wave you off, we'll need to move through fast."

"Yes, Coach," Alex said, joining Dane in the aisle.

Hartl pushed his way back to the front, through their teammates, who were up and about, gathering bags and peeking out the tinted windows.

Beside Alex, Dane held out his hand. "Give me mine first," he said. "I'm going out there with him. Let the press get it out of their system."

"Dane."

"Alejandro."

Their stare-down lasted all of five seconds, ending with Alex's defeated sigh. Bas lowered his chin, hiding his smile. He was still a little baffled and a lot amused at how easily Dane could chip through Alex's defenses with a few perfectly rolled syllables. In this case, though, it wasn't a complete Ellis victory.

Alex fished two passports out of the pouch, handed one to Dane, and kept the other for himself. "This is my team too," he said. "I'm going with you." He tossed the pouch to Bas. "You got this here?"

Bas nodded, and Alex followed Dane off the bus. The rest of the team rallied, grabbing their documents, shouldering bags, and joining Coach, Alex, and Dane in front of the gathered media.

Everyone except Jacob, who'd been unusually quiet during the long bus ride. He'd sat by himself in the row in front of Alex and Dane, declining Bas's invitation to join him in the back. Bas wondered if his refusal had to do with the way they'd woken up this morning, or if there was something else going on, maybe having to do with his hour-long disappearance right before go time.

Bas withdrew the last two passports and sank into the seat next to him, flipping through the blank pages in Jacob's booklet. "New passport?"

Jacob nodded, glancing over briefly before casting his gaze back down. Between his clasped hands, a shiny object momentarily blinded Bas.

"You lose your old passport?" Bas asked, squinting.

"That's my first one. This is my first time out of the country."

"Cool, first stamps." Bas wasn't surprised, given Jacob's age and relative obscurity on the swimming scene. A few of the younger athletes on the previous Olympic squad hadn't traveled abroad either before the Games. "We'll have to celebrate."

Except Jacob didn't appear in a celebratory mood. He turned the object—no, *objects*, two of them, dog tags—over and over in his hand, like his nerves from last night were resurfacing.

"Whose are those?" Bas asked.

The tumbling stopped, the metal tags faceup. Jacob ran a thumb across the name imprinted on them.

BURROWS, DAVIS J.
USMC.

Dread sank like a brick tied to Bas's ankles.
Fuck.

Did those tags belong to Jacob's father? Or to a brother, maybe? A relative, for sure, given the same last name. With the way Jacob was acting, was Davis dead? Killed in combat? Maybe on a flight? Shot down? That'd explain Jacob's sudden anxiety right before a transatlantic flight. "Jacob, I'm sor—"

Jacob's head whipped up, eyes meeting his. "No, no, no. He's still alive. My dad."

Bas breathed a small sigh of relief, but Jacob's down demeanor made even less sense now. "Pup, I don't get it."

"I went to see him, before we left. He gave me these, to . . ." Jacob shook his head, fingers closing around the tags. "For good luck. He's excited for me."

Bas lifted a hand to cup Jacob's cheek, to tease the tip of his frown into a smile, the instinct to comfort him easy and

35

natural. But after this morning, and given Jacob's present distress, Bas stopped himself short, clasping his shoulder instead. "Why aren't you? This is the Olympics."

Jacob shrugged. "I am excited. Worried too."

"We talked about this last night. We've got the gold locked up." Bas pointed out the window at Alex and Dane. "Just look at those two." Next to Coach, their team a united front behind them, Alex and Dane stood tall and proud, Dane's hand resting at the small of Alex's back as they answered questions. Not a sight Bas thought he'd ever see, but unquestionably right.

Jacob, however, didn't seem convinced that his worry was unnecessary, his eyes still locked on the dog tags. "I've never been this far away."

The sudden homesickness struck Bas as odd, nothing of the sort having come up in Colorado or Texas. Granted, San Antonio was Jacob's hometown, but he hadn't said a word about his family or actual home, until now. On second thought, maybe *that* was odd.

Was this the next page of Jacob's story?

Bas rewound Jacob's words. He'd said his father was *still alive*. Had something happened to him? Was that why Jacob was reluctant to leave? That would be the Jacob Bas had come to know—always putting others first. Too worried about his dad to be excited for the Olympic experience ahead.

"Jacob, is there something more?"

Outside, Alex glanced over his shoulder, searching the crowd, then peered over the heads of the gathered team to the bus. Their absence had been noticed, and Jacob apparently recognized the offered reprieve. He stood and loomed over Bas from the inside seat. "We need to go. They're waiting on us."

Answers would have to wait. Rising, Bas returned to his seat and gathered his things. He hastily donned his coat and tie and turned back around to see Jacob dragging his feet toward the exit.

Fuck waiting.

Three long strides and Bas caught up to him, gently clasped Jacob's elbow, and rotated him. "Whatever it is, Pup, you can tell me."

Jacob smiled as he pocketed the dog tags. "I'm good."

For the first time since they'd met, Bas saw Jacob's smile for what it was—a mask. Like Alex wore sometimes, except Jacob wore his better. "Hey," Bas said softly. "Remember how we told Alex he didn't have to take it all on himself? The same applies to you."

"I don't have nearly as much—"

"Jacob, the same applies to you." He squeezed Jacob's elbow for emphasis. "The Olympic experience is going to blow your mind. It will be overwhelming. You're strong, Pup. Stronger than any of us have given you credit for, I'm starting to think, but I guarantee, the weight and chaos will hit you. When it does, you come to me or Alex or Dane. Okay?"

Jacob's eyes grew wide, round mint dimes, as the clink of metal—Jacob turning the tags over in his pocket—echoed in the otherwise silent bus.

Bas slid his hand up Jacob's arm, grasping his biceps just below where the Longhorn tattoo hid beneath his sleeve. "I'm here."

The clink of metal stopped and red slashed across Jacob's cheeks, same as it had when Bas had yanked the curtain back in the tattoo shop. When he'd uttered those exact same words. Their eyes locked, no mirror for distance between them, and fuck if Jacob didn't look as beautiful now as he had then.

Beauty Bas wanted to touch. Desire blazed to life again, warring with his good intentions, twin flames racing through his veins. He'd wrecked beauty like this before, and not in the good way. He couldn't—*wouldn't*—do the same to Jacob. That was the very opposite of looking out for him.

He released Jacob's arm just as Sean thundered up the stairs. "Show's over," the distance swimmer called from the front. "You can come out now."

"On our way." Bas handed Jacob his passport and nudged him forward. "Was just keeping the pup safe from the vultures."

Jacob trotted ahead, descending the steps behind Sean. "Time to get some stamps," he said, voice chipper. But as they crossed the parking lot, Bas watched Jacob slip his hand back into the pocket with the dog tags.

Worry hidden, but still present.

Bas had gotten another page of the pup's story. He wasn't sure he liked it.

CHAPTER
FOUR

BITTE AND *ENTSCHULDIGUNG*—two German words Jacob learned on day one in Vienna. Since arriving yesterday, he'd lost count of how many times he'd heard the former. The Viennese used the German word for *please* like American college kids used, well, *like*. Far more useful was *Entschuldigung—excuse me*—the magic word for shoving his way out of the packed U-Bahn before the highly efficient, timed-to-the-second subway sped off.

Outside of the subway car, Burggasse Station was likewise swarming with morning commuters. Crowd size bigger than he was used to, German voices so very different from his everyday mix of English and Spanish, Jacob was more than a little disoriented. After a restless day and night thanks to jet lag, he admittedly wasn't in the best shape for an off-book excursion. He probably should have waited on his teammates, or at least dragged Sean, who'd studied abroad here, with him. But that'd defeat the purpose of getting a few extra minutes of peace before training chaos resumed.

By the time he got his wits about him, he'd been ferried by the crowd up the stairs to the street-level concourse.

Rather than exiting across the black-and-white-tiled foyer, he shouldered his bag and climbed another level to the exhibit hall. As soon as he set foot inside, he felt at home again. Here, in the quiet showroom full of old cars and motorcycles, he could practically smell the oil and grease, the same scents his dad brought home from the garage every day. Peace settling over him, Jacob looked his fill and snapped pictures to send home. Arranged like they were racing on a track, an impressive collection of Harleys led a pack of trailing motorcycles from all over the world. Inside the racing oval, there were a dozen or so more bikes on display, including several vintage US Army panheads and a couple of military transports. He was neck-deep in an old Volkswagen truck when a familiar voice called out "Pup" behind him.

He turned, grinning wide, and Bas smiled back. "I see you've found your favorite place in Vienna."

"My dad's a mechanic," Jacob explained. "Uncle owns the shop. I grew up around cars there, whenever Dad was home between tours."

"Home away from home, then." Bas held out a travel mug to him. "Now it's time for our other home, in the pool," he said, directing them toward the exit. At the top of the stairs he paused, asking, "You take plenty of pictures?"

"Tons." Jacob took a sip from the mug and nearly spit out the bitter liquid, scowling. "Is this shit rocket fuel?"

"Don't knock the Turkish coffee. You'll thank me later." Bas threw a wink over his shoulder, then started down the steps. "I load up on it whenever I travel to Europe for meets or whatnot. Jet lag cure-all. Alex would mainline it if he could."

Reminded again of his inexperience, Jacob's smile faltered. He didn't have long to dwell on it though, as Bas brought up a more urgent, equally unpleasant, topic.

"Got a text from Nat." Natalie Harris was the women's team captain and a former USC teammate of Alex and Bas. "Reporters outside the pool."

"Shit. They on about Alex and Dane?"

"They're asking about you, Pup."

Jacob gulped. "Me?"

"You and the rest of the new talent—Mike, Terrence, the other rooks. But we're not ready to reveal all our cards yet."

Jacob was beginning to think they were taking this secret-weapon thing too far. He understood the strategy—protect him and the other noobs, and also maintain a competitive advantage—but the pressure of living up to the hype they were building was mounting steadily. As was the guilt at needing "extra handling." The vets had enough on their plates already.

"I can handle it," Jacob said, not entirely convinced but bolstered by another giant gulp of rocket fuel.

Bas shook his head. "You, Dane, and the other rooks are going to break off a block early. One of Nat's squad will meet you at the facility's back entrance."

Before Jacob could object, they reached the bottom of the steps and the rest of the team. Bas walked ahead to join Alex and Sean, while Dane drew alongside Jacob. "You trying to show us up, beating us here early?"

Stymied, for now, Jacob turned his attention to Dane. "Wanted to check out the transportation museum." He pointed upstairs.

"Good stuff?"

"Yeah, lots of classic cars and bikes. You want to see pictures?"

"Heck yeah!"

He flipped through the pictures with Dane as the team walked up the street to the gleaming glass-and-metal aquatic complex ahead. Before arriving in the Olympic host city, many US teams practiced in other cities nearby—a final training push and a chance to get acclimated after travel. They could have trained closer to Madrid, in Barcelona with some of the other US teams, but USA Swimming had selected Vienna, Austria, for the competition-level Stadthallenbad aquatic complex.

And for the distance from the media swarming Spain.

Not that the media weren't out in force here too. A block from the pool, they could see the press gathered out front, just as Natalie had warned. Per the plan, the newbies, himself and Dane included, broke off and snuck in the back entrance. Once the heavy doors swung closed, the thick soup of chlorinated air wrapped around them like a safety blanket, the relief immense.

The same relief showed on the rest of their teammates' faces as they all met up outside the locker room to ditch their bags before the facility tour. Jacob tried hard not to look like an awestruck kid, and he was holding it together well. Until they entered the main event area. His jaw hit the deck as he struggled to take in the sheer enormity of the place. Industrial in design, it was a marvel of metal, glass, and water. Huge in area, a vaulted metal ceiling, buttressed by red metal struts, stretched the length of an eight-track pool. A long wall of floor-to-ceiling windows, plus elevated windows above the opposite-facing spectator stands, cast the cavernous space in bright morning light. And at either end of the pool, diving blocks, pacing clocks, and digital leaderboards fed swimmers and coaches all the info they could possibly need.

At the deep end, closest to where they'd entered, the divers were inspecting the multilevel platforms and springboards, while at the far end, the women's team mingled.

"Pretty cool, huh?" Sean said.

Jacob silently nodded, still grasping for words.

"Was a bitch of a reconstruction project," Sean carried on, as they made their way to the other end of the pool. "Only got to swim here for a summer before they shut it down. Was still closed when I moved on to Munich." Sean was getting a PhD in German studies from Emory. As part of his program, he'd studied here, Munich, and Berlin for two of the four years between this and the last Olympics.

"Well, hello, boys," Nat greeted. "Finally decided to show, huh?" Pulling her dyed-red curls into a bun, she flexed her toned brown arms, and Jacob was fairly certain they could squash him.

Alex, at the front of their group, held out his hand and went through a secret-society-level handshake with Nat. "You did get the closer dorms."

"Coaches must've thought you need the extra exercise,"

she joked.

"Oh, is that it?" Bas shouldered through and wrapped Nat in a bear hug, lifting her off her feet. "I think you just wanted the single rooms."

"Lies, all lies." She laughed and blew a raspberry on his cheek.

Jacob couldn't help but wonder if there was more than friendship between them, either in the past or present. Casually affectionate with each other and both still living in LA, Nat and Bas would make sense, their interests and locations aligning. Jacob's stomach did a funny flip, and he looked away, absently rubbing a hand over his tattoo.

"You ever seen anything like this place?" came a voice on his other side.

The rolling Baltimore accent gave away the speaker before Jacob even turned his head. Leah Franklin, the bubbly, twenty-one-year-old breaststroke champ from Maryland, was the women's team's social butterfly. So why the hell was the cute brunette talking to a dork like him? He ran a hand over his head, wondering if Josh had been right. Was a haircut and tattoo all it took to make him cool? No fucking way. Except Leah was looking up at him with an inviting smile and interested hazel eyes, waiting for an answer.

While he imitated a goldfish, opening and closing his mouth in startled surprise. *Words*, Josh coached in his head. *Words would be good.* He cleared his throat, forcing them out. "UT's natatorium is big, other complexes too, but this is huge, and everything here is so bright and shiny and—"

"Clean." She read his mind. "Like the airport and subways too."

"Yes! And our dorms at the academy are like five-star-hotel clean." Not that he'd ever been in one, but the graduate academy where they were lodging was the furthest thing from a school dorm Jacob had ever seen.

"I know, right?" Leah said. "The place we're staying at is the same!"

From there, they devolved into a bitch-fest about their UT and UMD dorms, until the coaches called everyone over to the bleachers. Rather than diverting down Nat's row, Leah followed him up a few rows, sitting close enough for their shoulders to brush. Climbing the stairs past them, Bas shot him an odd look—brow furrowed over narrowed eyes and his lips pressed together like he was holding in words. Jacob had never seen that expression on Bas's face before. He wanted to turn and get a better read on it, but Coach Hartl was banging the bottom bleacher for their attention.

"Welcome to the name of the place I can't pronounce," Hartl said.

"Stadthallenbad," Sean pronounced, his German perfect.

"Yeah, that," Coach muttered, talking over the laughing crowd. "All right, all right, let's focus now. It's just us here for the next five days. We'll alternate shifts between the three pools—women, men, and divers. Schedules are on the white boards in the locker rooms, and Alex will email 'em to you as well. Pool is open from 6 a.m. to 9 p.m. There's open swim time built into the schedule, but don't overdo it. And leave time for dry-land workouts back at the dorms. They've both got gyms."

"Morning runs start tomorrow," Sean called out. "Nat, meet us at Karlsplatz? Ass crack of dawn?"

"You got it," she replied with a wink. "Happy to smoke your ass any day."

"Good, that's settled," Coach said. "Any other questions?"

"I wanna hear you say the name of this place," Bas shouted, drawing another round of laughter.

Coach did not look amused, his black eyes glittering. "Shut it, Stewart, and take your crew to Pool Three. Divers start up here today."

"Ladies," Coach Albert, the women's team head said, "we're in Pool Two today." She blew her whistle, the sound echoing in the big open space.

Leah bumped her shoulder against Jacob's. "Can't say I've missed that sound the past couple days."

Jacob agreed, though he was more than game for what it signaled. After two days of travel and nothing but a run last night, he was ready to get back in the water. So was everyone else, judging by how fast his teammates jumped to it. Exiting into the aisle, Jacob started to step down but a colorful arm wrapped around his shoulders and hauled him back.

"Ladies first, Pup," Bas said, right next to his ear.

Grinning, Leah exited the row and offered a playful curtsey. "Thank you, gentlemen." Her gaze strayed briefly to Bas, before landing back on Jacob, eyes still sparkling with interest. For him, not Bas. How was that possible? Could she not see how gorgeous the man behind him was?

The man whose hold tightened and whose warm, hard

chest pressed flush against his back. "Time to work," Bas said, voice rumbling against Jacob's spine.

"You guys have a good swim," Leah said, her parting wave matching her flirty smile.

She was just out of earshot when, from somewhere behind Jacob, Dane observed, "If y'all are done flirting now . . ."

Jacob gulped, his lurching Adam's apple running into Bas's forearm. Did Dane mean Jacob and Leah, or Jacob and Bas? Had Bas told Dane, or Alex, about what happened at the tattoo parlor? About falling asleep together the other night?

Ahoy, Davy Jones! Walking the plank of mortification . . .

"With the ladies," Dane added, and Jacob covered his weak-kneed stumble out of Bas's loosening hold with a pirate quip about bonny lasses, since his brain had already gone there anyway.

They laughed the rest of the way into the locker room, until Dane hit the brakes in front of the whiteboard, and Jacob careened into his back.

"This is what you were doing last night?" Dane said to Alex.

Their captain's sharp, slanted handwriting was unmistakable.

"And you put medley relay in the pool first? Man, some boyfriend you are." Dane poked out his bottom lip, mischief dancing in his blue-gray eyes.

Three weeks ago, those same eyes had been cold and angry. Three weeks ago, Alex would not have responded by swatting Dane's ass, with a teasing, "Buck up, *gringo*."

They retrieved their bags from the pretour pile, then joined Sean and Mike in the first row of lockers, while Jacob settled across the aisle from them in the row with Bas and Kevin.

"Was that your dad you were on Skype with last night?" Bas asked. "I didn't mean to interrupt."

"No, it's okay. I'm the one who's sorry."

Bas had come in after a run, sped through a shower, and ducked back out before Jacob could flag him down. He'd only needed a few more minutes. He should have apologized last night or this morning—he didn't want Bas thinking he couldn't come and go to their shared room—but there'd been a million other things on Jacob's mind.

Bas sat on the bench, digging his cap and goggles out of his bag. "No worries. Took a walk, then hung out in the academy lounge."

"More *X-Files*?" The team obsession had started in San Antonio, a nightly wind down with Mulder and Scully.

"Two seasons left."

Jacob settled next to him, clawing through his own bag for the rest of his gear. "Hate to break it to you, but your time would be better spent on *Black Sails* at this point. Last two seasons of *The X-Files* suck donkey balls."

Bas gasped, hand to his chest and face drawn in exaggerated betrayal. "You've watched it already?" Jacob shrugged, smiling, and Bas's gasp turned into an answering grin. "Of course you have, dork."

No use denying it. Jacob laughed, liking that the guys on

his team were cool with his uncoolness. The girls too, it seemed. So fucking bizarre. Josh was never going to believe him.

"He doing okay? Your dad?" Bas asked, putting the skids on Jacob's amusement. "You were worried about him when we left Texas."

"Yeah, he's good." Jacob stood, zipped his bag, and shoved it into a locker. Or tried to at least, the bulky bag and narrow space foiling his efforts at deflection. Reaching an arm in, Bas helped squeeze the bag into the locker, and Jacob slammed the metal door closed. "That's fucking teamwork," Jacob singsonged.

Chuckling, Bas leaned a shoulder against the adjacent locker and dipped his head, catching Jacob's eyes. "I'm glad he's good, but if he's ever not"—his voice and face turned serious—"I'm here, if you need to talk. We're all here, Pup."

Kevin crossed behind them, on the other side of the bench, and held out a closed fist for a bump. "We've got your back, Pup, especially when things get wild in Madrid." Kevin's dark waggling eyebrows and gleeful expression were frightening in a Jack Torrance from *The Shining* sort of way.

Jacob glanced between his teammates. "Why does that not comfort me?"

Bas's knowing smirk was not exactly comforting either, even if his words were beautiful. "Don't worry, I'll protect you."

CHAPTER FIVE

THREE DAYS OF hard practice and Bas was impressed with what he saw in the pool. Medley relay was back to full speed with Alex in the lineup again, and the individual medley swimmers had also bounced back after losing Ryan. Terrence, now their lead IM swimmer and also Jacob's breaststroke backup, was within a couple hundredths of Ryan's personal best, and their third IM swimmer, Hunter, Bas's fly backup, was only a few tenths behind him. Both men's and women's teams had rallied behind them, cheering whenever they were in the pool, frustrating Coach as he tried to track the swimmers with his stopwatch, no matter the giant clocks at either end.

Midway up the bleachers, Bas had a better view than all of them, which Alex had recognized too, frequently ditching the pool-side ruckus and joining him with a notebook. Today, though, the captain's hands were free as he shuffled down the row toward Bas.

"Any new designs you love?"

Alex was used to him sketching at all hours, including during practice, the waterproof graphics tablet making it even easier to draw on deck than it used to be. His sketches usually made it onto his, a teammate's, or a client's skin, or onto his LA shop's walls. The drawings in this folder, however, were for Bas's eyes only. Tablet angled so Alex couldn't see the screen, Bas saved and closed the drawing, sliding it into the folder labeled *DPR*.

"Working it out," Bas said, as he set the tablet aside. Changing the subject, he jutted his chin at the pool. "Terrence and Hunter are doing well; you'd be doing better." While Alex raced in medley relay and backstroke, he was a gifted all-around swimmer. Almost as good as Ryan in IM.

Alex shook his head. "That's the last thing I want to do after what went down with Ryan. It'd only prove his point." Ryan had been angry at the veterans, like Alex and Bas, who'd returned to take up starting spots again on the squad. "I'm not about to take his one spot, or the two for that matter."

"I don't think the rest of the team would see it that way if you're the most qualified."

Alex looked out over the pool, then back at him. "Have you heard any similar discontent from the younger swimmers?"

"Not me, but let's go to the source." Bas cupped his hands around his mouth and shouted, "Yo, Pup!"

Jacob popped up from where he'd been kneeling by the pool next to Terrence, cheering on and coaching his backup. Selfless, perhaps to a fault, in a sport that required competitive drive. Was this why Jacob "didn't know how to win"?

Did he really choke or was he putting himself second? Letting others take the spotlight instead? Bas would have to talk to him; that mindset would not fly at the Olympics, especially with other swimmers trying to get in his head. For now, though, they had to deal with their own squad's bigger issues. He waved over the youngest member of their team.

"Ahoy!" Jacob plopped down on the bleacher row in front of them. "What's up?"

"Any more rumblings from the greenhorns about us vets?" Bas asked, returning a little sailor speak.

"Matey!" Jacob said, holding out a fist for a bump.

Bumping back, Bas laughed, indulging in Jacob's big toothy smile, until Captain Alex brought them to task. "English or Spanish, no pirate please."

Still smiling, Jacob returned to attention, following his captain's orders. "Mike watches you two"—he gestured at Alex and Bas—"and Kevin and Sean, like a hawk. He swam with Ryan at Florida, so I thought maybe he'd be a problem, but I caught a glimpse of his journal the other night in the lounge, and it's full of swim notes. He's not resentful at all, just eager to learn. Looking to you vets for expertise." Jacob rattled off several more hyperobservant tidbits about their teammates that would have made a shrink, or detective, proud.

"You got all that, just observing?" Alex said, shaking his head. "That CompSci degree you're getting is wasted. You should have gone into psych."

"Cousin's the psych major," Jacob said with a shrug. "I pick things up." More than a few things, Bas judged.

"Honestly," Jacob continued, "we're all too focused on the now and terrified about what to expect next."

"In Madrid?" Alex said.

Jacob nodded. "We've heard the stories. How do we keep our focus with all that craziness going on?"

"You've all been to meets before."

"Yeah, but this is the *Olympics*." Jacob made a huge sweeping motion with his arms, almost losing his balance, then laughing at himself with Alex and Bas. After a moment, he added more seriously, "No one wants to let the team down." The *no one* was a clear substitution for *I*, consistent with the concerns he'd expressed to Bas in San Antonio. Those doubts and worries obviously still lingered, because what lay ahead was unknown. But what if it could be known? Or at least simulated? An idea sparked in Bas's mind that continued to take root as Alex and Jacob chatted.

"We're just trying to keep our heads down and swim," Jacob said.

"You'll let me know if anything changes?"

Jacob stood, saluting. "Aye, aye, Captain."

Leah met him at the bottom of the steps, looping an arm through his. "Saw you giving Terrence some turn tips. Think you might share with us too?"

Jacob grinned at her, cheeks slightly pinked. "Yeah, sure."

"We're in the water in ten, Pup," Bas said. "Don't get too distracted."

Jacob shot another smile over his shoulder, as Leah tugged him forward. Bas tracked them all the way around to the other side of the pool, where Jacob jumped in with Leah and several of the other women, a mini-splash fest ensuing.

"You still know what you're doing there?" Alex asked low.

Bas repeated his answer from San Antonio, "Not doing anything," even as his memories played like a film reel of contradictions. The tattoo parlor; waking up with Jacob in his arms; watching him sleep every night, the pup's light snores endearing.

"That look on your face doesn't say 'Not doing anything.'"

Bas schooled his blasted features and swung his eyes back to Alex. "I made you a promise. I intend to keep it."

"Are the two things mutually exclusive?"

Bas lost control of his features again, surprise reigning. Was Alex suggesting what Bas thought he was? "You were there four years ago. You've got a medley relay silver in your case at home instead of gold." He pointed at his chest. "My fault."

"We were all distracted, Sebastian."

"Because of what I did. Not doing that again."

Alex tilted his head, dark eyes searching. "If I'm reading this right, you'll do anything *not* to hurt the pup, which worries me almost as much."

"How about you look after your own first timer, and I'll look after mine?"

"Yours, huh?"

He'd stepped right into that one. "You baited me, motherfucker."

Alex lifted a brow, giving him a so-what-if-I-did face that morphed into a soft smile when his wandering gaze landed on Dane.

"How are things going with your first timer?" Bas asked.

"A little unreal still. It's such a one-eighty."

No argument there. Dane had gone from repressed and fuming, to competing with Jacob for head cheerleader. Out of the pool, Dane was permanently attached to his boyfriend; he couldn't keep his hands off Alex. "Maybe he's making up for lost time." Ten years of it. "You're happy?"

"I got what I thought I never would, so yeah, I'm beyond happy."

"And after Madrid?"

Alex shifted on the bleacher, angling toward Bas. "Been meaning to talk to you about that." Words that rarely preceded anything good. A knot formed in Bas's gut. Had he been so stuck in his own head that he'd missed some sign of distress in Alex? Was his best friend's well-earned happiness already in jeopardy?

Bas couldn't have been more wrong.

"Once Mom's done with her chemo and feeling better, Dane and I were considering giving LA a shot, if you think your club would still have us. I miss it out there and swimming with you."

Warmth expanded in Bas's chest, dissolving the knot of worry. "I think the club would be more than happy to have you and Big Red." He slung an arm over his best friend's shoulders, hugging him. "And so would I."

CHAPTER
SIX

BAS HAD SPIED Martin's the first day they'd arrived in Vienna. From the back seat of the van that took them to the academy, he'd craned his neck to check out the pub with the Irish and Union Jack flags out front. Later, when Jacob had been on the phone with his dad, Bas had gone for a walk around town and drifted into the establishment, lured by the waft of fried chicken and nineties grunge music. The oddities continued inside, namely a merry Australian lumberjack behind the bar. An Irish/English pub, in Austria, that played American music, served American food, and was run by Australians. The mishmash was perfect, reminding Bas of home, and Ernie, the brawny barkeep and owner, wasn't too hard to look at either.

The auburn-haired highlander clone slid a basket of chicken nuggets and a pint of hard cider onto the bar in front of Bas. "Brought the whole team tonight, did ya?" Ernie's words and face were cheerful, not at all bothered by the horde of athletes invading his pub.

Pushing aside his napkin sketch, Bas laid down the pen he'd stolen from behind the bar and took a swallow of the cold, bittersweet brew, bubbles of sharp citrus bursting on his tongue. "Idea I had at practice today," he said.

Martin's was a scene at night, and a good trial run for the sort of chaos his teammates would face in Madrid. A training exercise to practice how they'd behave out of the pool in the face of temptation. "Give them a measured taste," he'd pitched to Alex. "See how they handle it."

Alex and Nat had talked it over and gotten their respective coaches' approvals, with two ground rules—midnight curfew and a two-drink limit. Alex, Bas, Nat, and Eva, the women's second, were limited to one drink each. They needed to stay sober and observe, watching out for the flagrant rule breakers and also those who might be swayed to do so by inexperience or the need to fit in.

"So far so good," Ernie said. "They seem to be enjoying themselves."

"I'm sure the familiar music and these—" he picked up a nugget "—help. Just like home." He popped one into his mouth, smiling.

Ernie chuckled. "When do you leave for Madrid?"

"Two more days of practice, then travel day."

The bartender unwrinkled Bas's doodled-on napkin and scribbled a number on the back. "You get to feeling lonesome before Sunday, you know where to find me." He pushed the napkin under Bas's nose, then threw him a flirtatious wink as he shimmied his bubble butt to the other end of the bar. Not a bad view at all.

Grabbing his pint glass, Bas spun on his stool and rested back against the bar, sipping his cider and tracking the team around the pub. Natalie, Sean, and several others were huddled in two front-window booths; Alex was presiding over a pop-up billiards tournament in the other front corner; and in the back, to the right of the bar, Eva stood on the border of the dance floor, monitoring their swimmers bouncing and swaying to the music, including Jacob.

His spiky blond hair refracted the dance floor lights as he threw himself into a white-boy head-bob, not an ounce of rhythm in his movements. Leah didn't seem put off in the slightest, laughing and lifting on her toes to shout at him over the music. Bas hid his scowl behind the rim of his glass. Of course she wouldn't be put off; Jacob was adorable in his guileless enthusiasm. And Bas had no right to begrudge Jacob a shot at someone who appreciated him just the way he was. They seemed genuinely interested in each another, spending more and more time together, in and out of the pool. Maybe it was a summer fling, or maybe it would develop into more. With that thought sitting like an elephant on his chest, Bas drained his cider and spun back around.

Not long after, Alex sidled up next to him, flagging Ernie down for a soda.

"You're the captain, right?" Ernie's good-humored smile stretched into a leer as he handed Alex a Coke bottle. "Seen you on TV. You and Red over there"—he gestured at Dane—"need a third while you're in town, I'm game."

"Fucker!" Bas exclaimed in mock protest, tossing a balled-up napkin at him. "You hit on me not five minutes ago."

"Can you blame me? My bar is crawling with hot athletes. I'm gonna keep shootin' darts until one of 'em lands." Leaning forward, he braced his freckled forearms on the bar. "So, what do you say, Captain?"

Alex smiled, looking not the least bit put off. "Appreciate the offer, but we'll pass."

Bas had lost count of how many times he and Alex had been propositioned together in LA. When Natalie had shown up their junior year and started hanging out with them, she'd been a welcome third on their going-out adventures, making it appear they were an established throuple. In reality, it'd only ever been friendship among the three of them, but the mistaken impression of more took the pressure off in clubs.

"Shame," Ernie said, shaking his head. "Wasted two darts that time."

"Keep slinging 'em," Bas said. "You'll hit something."

Snickering, Ernie moved on to another customer, and Alex shot Bas a curious side-eye. "You didn't take him up on his offer?"

"Not really in the mood."

A crease formed between Alex's dark brows, his lips pressing together.

Bas knew that look well. "Spit it out, Cantu, whatever it is."

Alex pulled his phone out of his pocket. "This probably isn't going to improve your mood." He sat the device on the bar, faceup between them.

On the screen was a friend request with a picture of a

face Bas had done everything in his power to avoid the past four years. Since the last Olympics, when Bas had been a selfish, immature ass and hurt both his team and a man he'd cared for. The same man smiling up at him from Alex's phone. He'd grown into his striking features—a headful of thick black hair, green-gold eyes, and a strong square jaw that balanced out his pronounced nose and made the overall impression sharp and handsome.

"He's on the Spanish team again," Alex said. "He'll be in Madrid."

Bas propped his elbows on the bar and scrubbed his hands over his face. This wasn't a surprise; Bas had reckoned he'd be there. One of the top swimmers at USC with Alex and Bas, he'd been projected to win gold for Spain in his individual races at the last Olympics, before Bas had sent them both off the rails. With the Games in his home country this time, of course he'd be back. Of course Bas would have to face his biggest mistake while struggling not to make another.

"You mind running interference?" he said to Alex.

"Count on it."

"I didn't realize you hadn't stayed in touch."

"You're my best friend, even when you act like an idiot. And no real reason to, once he moved back across the pond."

Because Bas hadn't given him a reason to stay.

Stay.

His eyes strayed again to the dance floor. Jacob had asked him to stay and Bas had. In the tattoo parlor, on the bus, in the locker room. He'd promised to stay by his side throughout this Olympic experience, as a friend, teammate, and mentor. Had he also promised more? In his actions? In his heart? Bas wasn't sure which frightened him most—Jacob's possibly skewed expectations or his own definitely skewed desire to meet them knowing it'd only end in disaster.

Same as it had four years ago.

Bas rubbed a hand across his chest, over the lone tattoo, as he tried and failed not to make comparisons. Going down that road was dangerous, but it was also a necessary reminder of his mistakes.

That was the point of tonight, wasn't it? To get the mistakes out of the way. And would that third pint Mike was holding out to Jacob be the pup's first mistake?

Bas was half off the stool when Alex grabbed his arm.

"Give him a chance to make the right decision," Alex said.

Which Jacob did, waving Mike off with a good-natured smile.

"See," Alex said, releasing Bas's arm, "we don't have to worry about the pup. Between my boyfriend's hazing and your tattoo night out, I think he got his fill in San Antonio."

Bas focused on the former instead of the latter. "I think you also like saying that word *boyfriend*."

Alex's shy smile was all the answer Bas needed. For all the press attention and big announcements, it was the small everyday affections between Alex and Dane that made Bas happy for his friend. Alex deserved that, more than anyone Bas knew.

"Alejandro," Dane called from the pool tables. "I'm over

here making bets on your behalf."

Alex rolled his eyes. "*Ay Dios.*"

Chuckling, Bas returned the earlier side-eye. "Hope you're still as good at running the table as you were in college."

"Better," Alex said with a wink, before draining his soda and cutting back across the pub.

Rotating on his stool, Bas made another visual sweep of the place. Nat's crew in the booths were playing beer pong with soda caps, Sean's flirt turned way up. Alex and Dane had the pool tables under control, starting up another tourney round. And Eva was making laps around the dance floor, stopping for small talk while keeping a watchful eye out.

With Eva's attention on the group as a whole, Bas zeroed in on Jacob. Hair shiny and skin glistening with sweat, he played the part of carefree new adult well, bouncing with Leah and the others on the dance floor. Just a goofy college kid in his goofy *Walk the Plank* T-shirt having a fun night.

With the girl he maybe liked.

Probably liked.

Scowling, Bas started to turn back to the bar, when out of the corner of his eye, he noticed a shift in his favorite subject. And not a good one. Jacob was no longer having fun. Carefree mask ripped away, Jacob stared down at the phone in his hand and his skin blanched under the flashing lights. The next instant, he was shoving through the crowd toward the back exit.

Bas was moving before he made the decision to follow.

Hell, there was no decision to make. He'd made a promise—to look out for Jacob—regardless of what that might entail. He wove quickly through the thinner crowd around the outer edge of the dance floor. Reaching the back door before Leah, Bas waved her off and pushed through the door.

Outside in the alley, he heard Jacob before he saw him, ten or so feet ahead on the left, pacing the width of the narrow cobblestone street with his phone to his ear. Speaking fast, his voice was high and thready, alarmed. "He was fine when I talked to him earlier."

In his other hand, Jacob tumbled the dog tags as fast as his words, and Bas reckoned the *he* Jacob referred to must be his dad.

"Josh, what the fuck happened in just a few hours?"

The angry curse startled Bas. He'd only ever heard Jacob sound that short, seen his rangy body that puffed up, when they'd confronted Ryan back in San Antonio. That confrontation had ended with Jacob taking Ryan down in an impressive martial arts move. It sounded like that's what Jacob wanted to do to Josh right about now too. Was Josh the cousin he'd mentioned earlier, the psych major? And what did that have to do with Davis?

Bas was starting to put the pieces together, when, at the end of the alley, Jacob made a U-turn and lifted his head, spotting Bas for the first time. He froze midstep, eyes widening and nostrils flaring, reacting like a trapped animal. Standing in place, Bas raised his hands, palms out. He just wanted Jacob to know he was here if Jacob needed him.

Jacob hesitated a second, then whatever Josh said on the

other end of the line must have been more distressing than Bas's presence. He resumed his pacing, and Bas leaned a shoulder against the wall, out of Jacob's way but still there for him. Not leaving him alone.

"He needs to go to the clinic," Jacob said, then after a beat, "Yes, yes, put him on the line." He pocketed the tags and braced his hand against the wall, angled slightly away from Bas. "Hey, Dad," he said, voice wiped clean of anger, eerily flipped to calm and upbeat. To see him though, was a different story. Back straight, shoulders tight, and jaw clenched, the pup was barely holding it together. "No, no, it's no trouble. Tell me about work today."

The psychology of the cue was impressive. Jacob hadn't directly asked how his dad was doing or how he was feeling. Instead, he'd offered an innocuous prompt, aimed at getting to the details and series of events he wanted to know more about. Bas employed similar tactics at the tattoo shop and had tried the same on Jacob, to no avail.

This was more of the pup's story than Bas had ever gotten before.

Bas could tell when Jacob's father reached the part of the story Jacob wanted to know. Or maybe didn't want to know. Inhaling sharply, the pup curled in on himself, spine bowing like he'd been punched in the gut.

Bas couldn't take the distance any longer. Clearing his throat to signal his approach, he stepped across the alley and put a hand to Jacob's curved back. Jacob startled at first, then leaned into the touch, chasing it. Bas flattened his palm against Jacob's spine, cementing the connection and support.

"What do you want to do about that?" Jacob asked his dad, and after a moment, nodded. "Good, that should help you rest. And I'll call Doc." Davis's objection was so loud Bas could hear it. "Okay, okay, not tonight," Jacob cajoled. "You'll call in the morning. And you have your support group tomorrow evening. You're going to that, right?" Whatever answer Davis gave caused Jacob to relax, a little, the tension slowly ebbing from his frame. "Good, call me after." There must have been a handoff on the other end, Josh coming back on the line. "Can you stay there tonight, cuz?" Jacob asked, relaxing a little more into Bas's touch, closer to his body. "Great, thank you, and I'm sorry I snapped at you earlier. That was uncalled for."

They exchanged a few more words before Jacob ended the call. He shoved off the wall, forcing Bas back a step so he could spin and slump against the stone, hands clutching for hair that was no longer there.

Bas rested a shoulder next to him, close but not touching. "Tell me about your dad's day," he said, using Jacob's own method.

For a change, Jacob cut right to the chase. "My dad's a combat vet," he said, arms falling to his sides. "Afghanistan. Came home with PTSD."

"That's why you were worried about leaving," Bas said, connecting the dots. Jacob nodded. But there was still a piece missing. "What about your mom? She's not in the picture?"

His scruff-covered jaw clenched again. "She split five years ago," he gritted out. "I asked her to stay, to give him more time and to help me, but she couldn't handle it anymore. We've been on our own since."

Jacob's words from the tattoo parlor rattled around Bas's head. And heart.

"I put myself first once. It didn't end well."

A fourteen-year-old kid dealing with his father's postwar trauma. Everything aligned—the hyperobservation, putting others first, never asking for what he needed. Because the one time he had asked, he'd been left behind, by his own mother, to fend for himself and take care of his father.

"Christ," Bas hissed. "That's why you went to UT? To stay close?"

"I'm lucky they have a top-notch swim program." Jacob pushed off the wall and resumed his pacing, hands flailing as he spoke. "He hasn't had a flashback in over two years. Not a single one since Josh and I have been at UT." His words tumbled faster and faster, as did the dog tags in his hand. "But then I leave, to where I can't get back, to where I can't be there for him when he needs me. He gave me these—" he brandished the tags "—to keep me safe, but he's the one who needs them. I should be keeping him safe, but I'm a fucking ocean away and I can't!" His gaze bounced around the alley as his breaths grew shorter and thinner, on the verge of hyperventilating.

Bas moved in front of him, cutting off his circuit. "Pup, you need to take a second and breathe."

Jacob's chest rose and fell faster, green eyes filling with panic. Not on the verge, then; already gone. Bas stepped closer, and Jacob slammed into reverse, backing into the wall. Bas kept coming, not letting up. He lifted his hands and grasped the sides of Jacob's face, holding him steady.

"Breathe, Jacob," he coached.

Mint green dimes snapped to him, but Jacob's breaths were still too fast and short. His brain needed to move past the panic so his body could fall in line.

"Your dad's okay now?" Bas asked.

Jacob nodded. A short inhale.

"Your cousin, Josh, is taking care of him?"

He nodded again. Another short inhale.

"Josh is a psych major, right? You said that the other day."

"Yeah," he wheezed. "Aunt's also a nurse."

"Okay, someone's got your father, then. Multiple someones." Bas inched closer, bodies brushing as his thumbs swept over Jacob's cheeks. "Your dad's gonna be fine. He's safe, and so are you. I've got you, you're not alone, but I need you to breathe, baby."

Jacob's eyes fluttered closed as he choked on a strangled breath.

"You can do it," Bas said. "Just like we do in the water. In and out." Bas exaggerated his own breathing so Jacob could feel the rise and fall of his chest, could hear the exchange of air, could mirror both with his own.

Finally, Jacob began gulping air, his swimmer's instincts enough to break through the panic. One, two, three big inhales, followed by measured exhales.

Bas continued to breathe with him until Jacob's chest no longer heaved. "That's got it," he said, moving to step back.

Jacob's hands shot up and wrapped around Bas's wrists,

holding him in place. When Jacob's eyes opened, they were no longer brimming over with panic. They were the warmest shade of cool green Bas had ever seen. Molten mint. Impossible, and yet right there in front of him, scorching.

As was the single word that passed through his parted lips. "Stay."

Not scorching.

Wrecked.

Like he had been in that tattoo parlor.

A wave of heat, blazing off Jacob, slammed into Bas.

"Stay," Jacob whispered again, rougher and more urgent.

The plea raked down Bas's spine, making him tremble with things he shouldn't want. Things he shouldn't do. Others had left Jacob. He'd leave Jacob; it's what Bas did. It's what he'd done before, hurting someone he'd cared about and costing his team the gold. This, if he closed the distance between himself and Jacob, would be a terrible repeat. He'd be breaking his promises, to Alex and to Jacob, acting in no one's best interest.

But *fuck*, with Jacob looking at him like that, crooked teeth digging into his full lower lip, and sounding like that, a plea on a whimper, Bas felt the pull all the way to his balls.

Jacob like this—like always—was beauty Bas couldn't turn away from, same as in the tattoo parlor.

He rationalized away the rational; even if he couldn't make it better for Jacob in the long run, he could make it better for him now. Jacob needed him to stay. To make him forget all that worry, at least for the span of a kiss. Bas wanted to help, to comfort, and he wanted to taste that beauty.

Desperately.

He tightened his grip on Jacob's face, palms scraping against Jacob's scruffy jaw, the short hairs at the nape of Jacob's neck tickling his fingertips. Bas drew him in, erasing the distance between them, chests pressed together and other parts hardening, until they were maddeningly close.

Jacob's eyes fluttered closed again. "Bas," he breathed, the motion brushing their lips together.

Bas shifted his head, angling for more than a mere brush.

A taste of beauty, of Jacob, was so close.

Then so far away.

The pub door slammed open behind them, and Bas shot out of Jacob's hold, stumbling backward across the alley. His back hit the opposite wall just as Dane came around the open door.

"Hey! Alex wanted me to check on you two. We're getting ready to head back to the academy."

Hands behind his back, Bas clawed at the cold stone wall, trying to scour away the enticing sensation of rough stubble and warm skin. He cleared his throat, hoping his voice didn't sound as strangled as other parts of him felt. "You good, Pup?"

"Yeah, fine," Jacob said, heading for the door. "Had to take a family call."

"Everything okay?" Dane asked.

Jacob paused over the threshold, shooting a smoldering, inviting look at Bas. "It will be."

When he was sure his body wouldn't betray him, Bas

unglued himself from the wall, only to meet a wall of red-headed Southern nosiness. "Not your problem, Big Red."

"You're Alex's best friend. You're on his team. His problems are my problems."

Bas liked that for Alex, but not so much for himself right now.

"You turned out all right, Ellis," he said, deflecting. With Dane momentarily stunned, Bas slipped inside past him. Up front, Alex was herding the team toward the exit. "Go back to your man," Bas told Dane when he caught up. "I'm right behind you."

Waiting at the bar, Bas watched as Leah hovered close to Jacob, the two of them shuffling along with the departing crowd. The pup smiled at her, making some assurance or other, his easygoing mask back in place. For her sake, never for his own. Bas wanted to go after him, to tear away that mask and give Jacob a safe place to let the truth out, to find a true calm instead of an affected one, but his common sense had returned. Bas knew where those intentions would lead—to anything but safe. He couldn't do that—not to Jacob, not to Alex, and not to his team.

He did right instead and climbed onto an empty barstool.

"Not going back with the team?" Ernie asked.

"Not yet."

"Another cider, or something stronger?"

"Stronger."

Though Bas doubted even the strongest thing here would wipe from his mind those molten green eyes or that needy whimper.

CHAPTER
SEVEN

JACOB STOOD IN the corner of the L-shaped, on-deck cubby tower, waiting on a call from Josh. Seven hours ahead of Texas, he'd forced himself, against every instinct, not to text until afternoon Central European Time. Josh had texted right back that Jacob's dad needed to check in with his doctor first. That was thirty minutes ago, and Jacob was about to crawl out of his skin waiting for an update. With only five minutes until afternoon practice, the call window was closing, fast. If Jacob had to get in the water while still in the dark about his dad, he'd be even more useless than he'd been this morning.

Two words into another text and his phone finally vibrated, Josh's face filling the screen. Time short, Jacob didn't waste it on greetings. "How's Dad today? Did he sleep? What did Doc say?"

"Yo, cuz, chill. Everything's fine." His cousin sounded relaxed, like he was kicked back at the kitchen table enjoying his morning coffee.

Jacob tried not to sound as if he wanted to strangle him. "Yo, cuz, details."

"Yeesh," Josh muttered, and Jacob knew he'd failed. "Uncle D settled after you talked to him yesterday. Ate fine, took one of his pills, and passed out in his chair watching the Astros get clobbered by the Giants."

"Did he sleep through the night?"

"All the way. I was on the couch, across the room from him."

Guilt washed over Jacob, his murderous impulses quelled. If Josh was kicked back this morning, he deserved it after a night on that lumpy old sofa.

"No more nightmares," Josh added, and Jacob breathed a sigh of relief.

It'd been a nightmare that had set Davis off yesterday. He'd dozed in the garage office, a nightmare took hold, and when the new shop guy had tried to shake him awake, new guy found himself on the floor.

Jacob had made that mistake once, right after his dad had returned home from his last tour, when none of them realized how bad it had been. Jacob had wound up on the floor too. Josh's dad had pulled Davis off with seconds to spare before he ran out of breath. Jacob suspected that had been the beginning of the end for his mother, having to scream across the street for her brother-in-law to come save her kid. After a year of ups and downs, medicines that had caused manic and depressive episodes, and nightly fights over money and therapy that Jacob had heard through the walls, she'd left. Jacob had seen the wear on her—he'd felt it too, understood it was hard—but he'd been terrified of taking on his father's recovery alone, at thirteen, so he'd asked her for what he'd needed. To give his father a little more time. To stay for him. She'd told Jacob he could come with her, but Jacob wouldn't leave his father, the hero who'd done more than his share to keep him and their country safe.

"I want to talk to him," Jacob said.

"Can't. Uncle D's in the shower, and you should wait until the scheduled time later."

Head bowed, hand wrapped around the back of his neck, Jacob paced a circle around the tiny corner. "What's he doing today?"

"Doc cleared him to go to work."

"You sure that's the best thing?"

"Burrows!" Coach hollered behind him. "You know the rules. No calls on deck."

Jacob muted the phone and glanced over his shoulder. After his miserable showing this morning, the last thing Jacob wanted to do was draw more of Hartl's ire. "Family emergency," he said. "Just need to be sure it's settled."

Coach's irritation dissolved into concern. "You need more time?"

"No, I'll just be another minute. I'm sorry."

"Pup, if you need—"

Jacob shook his head. "It'll be fine, Coach."

"Don't start that shit with me. I've already got 'Mr. I'm Fine' over there," he said, jutting a thumb at Alex.

Jacob couldn't help but laugh. "My cousin's handling it," he said, some of his tension easing. "But with the time difference, I just got ahold of him."

"Okay then, finish up," Coach said, walking on by.

"Medley relay's up first."

Unmuting the line, Jacob brought the phone back to his ear. "Sorry, Coach interrupted."

"You need to go?" Josh said.

"Yeah, and you and Doc are right about the routine, with work and the calls. I'm sorry. I'm just . . . out of sorts, being unable to help from here."

"It's fine, cuz. I understand it's frustrating." He really had no idea, but Jacob appreciated the sentiment, and his cousin's patience. "Uncle Beau's going to keep a close watch at the shop today." Beau was the third brother and owner of the garage where Jacob's dad worked. "You'll call Davis after your practice, and I'll take him to his support group tonight after dinner."

Jacob ran a hand over his head, as relieved as he could be under the circumstances. "Okay, thanks. Call or text if there's a problem."

"There won't be."

Jacob hoped like hell he was right. They finished up, and Jacob shoved his phone, towel, and flops in his designated cubby.

"Yo, Pup," Kevin said, coming around the side of the cubby tower with Sean. "What's up with your boy today?"

"My boy?"

Kevin nodded toward Bas at the other end of the pool, and Jacob prayed he didn't blush too noticeably. Was his crush on Bas that obvious? Or had Dane seen more than he'd let on last night and told others on the team?

"Your mentor," Kevin went on. "He wasn't at morning

practice or lunch, and now he's stomping around like an angry tattooed bear."

Jacob tried not to look too relieved, or too confused, as he eyed Bas *stalking* the far end of the pool. There was no other word for it. Gone was the ever-present tablet, Bas's fingers white-knuckling goggles and a cap instead. Gone were his relaxed shoulders and easy bearing, his body rigid and his gait jerky. Gone was his smile and laid-back manner, replaced with a virtual thundercloud over his head and a storm brewing in his blue eyes.

Approach with caution.

Or more accurately, *Do Not Approach.*

"I don't think he came back to the academy last night," Mike said, joining their slow stroll to the other end of the pool. "His key was still at the security desk this morning when we left to run."

"Did he, Pup?" Sean asked.

All their eyes swung to Jacob.

"I don't know," he lied. "I was out pretty hard after we got back."

The rumor was true; Bas hadn't come back last night. Jacob had stayed awake into the wee hours, waiting for Bas to accept the invitation he'd thrown out there in the alley, then worrying when it became clear he wasn't going to. Add to that the heavy guilt of leaving his father and the swirling doubts over competing in Madrid, and he'd felt like a castaway on a rickety ocean raft—hopeless, nauseous, and frustrated without even a volleyball to squawk to. They were two days from the Olympics, and everything was unravelling.

And it was all his fault.

"I saw him flirting with that bartender at the pub," Kevin said, as they huddled to a stop.

"According to Ryan," Mike said, "he broke up with his boyfriend at the start of the last Olympics, then fucked his way through the next two weeks, women *and* men."

Kevin nodded. "That's the reason they silvered in medley relay. Bas and his ex, Team Spain's rock star who also swam at USC, got into a big fight opening night. Bas was out with someone new that night and every night after. Alex covered for him, but they were still off. Fucked the other guy up worse. He was the favorite in his events and didn't medal at all."

"Dude's a fucking legend," Sean said, jutting his chin at Bas. "Women and men lining up. I expect no less this go round, especially since he's been a monk all through training."

"Until last night," Kevin said with a leer.

Jacob's stomach did another of those awful flips, nowhere near as graceful as the somersault a diver made off the platform to his right. When Bas hadn't returned last night, he'd convinced himself that Bas had crashed in the lounge or in Alex and Dane's room, not accepting his invitation and not wanting to make him feel embarrassed. Jacob could explain away the near-kiss as comfort offered, then reined back in. But apparently Bas hadn't been thinking of him at all. Hearing he'd accepted someone else's invitation, and about Bas's popularity at the last Games, reminded Jacob where he ranked—at the very back of a very long line he'd stupidly and ineptly tried to butt into. He'd made a fool of himself—grabbing Bas's wrists, holding him close, and asking for too much. Awkward Jacob was making things awkward, *surprise*, and jeopardizing the squad's chance at relay gold because he wanted . . . what with Bas—a kiss, a hookup, more?

Sean elbowed him, jostling him out of his sinking thoughts. "Works out for you and Leah. Room to yourself."

Jacob shook his head. "She's nice, but we're just friends."

"She wants to be more than *just friends* with you," Kevin said.

Heads swung as they checked out the women's team across the pool. Leah was staring right at Jacob, eyeing him with flirtatious interest. Close in age, they had similar interests, more than just swimming and breaststroke in common, and Leah's bubbly personality was a pleasant distraction. Jacob liked hanging out with her, and she seemed to like hanging out with him too, against all odds. She even got his stupid jokes, or at least pretended to. He could see their friendship continuing after the Games. But more? The last thing he wanted to do was lead Leah on, because if he had a shot with Bas . . . But did he? What was the sense in pushing after his bumbling foul last night? When he wasn't even on Bas's radar? But he was on Leah's. Would he drop off it, though, when she realized he was bi? Or that he was a super uncool virgin?

Mike slapped his shoulder. "Now he's thinking."

"Maybe don't think too hard yet," Kevin said, laughing. "You'll have your pick of chicks when we get to Madrid."

Or dudes.

Coach blew his whistle before Jacob could correct them. Not that he would, yet. He wasn't closeted, but the team was already dealing with enough drama and press attention without him causing more.

"Medley relay's first," Hartl shouted. "Rest of you fools out of the water."

"Let's roll, ladies!" Coach Albert shouted, rounding up her squad to go to Pool Two.

Leah waved as they walked past. "Have a good practice, Jacob."

"You too," he replied, on his way to the blocks where Dane was giving Alex a hand down into the water, Bas standing off to the side.

"What was that about?" Bas asked, storm still raging in his eyes.

The heavy, humid air did nothing to chase away the chill that crept up Jacob's spine. "She was just saying hi."

"Not her," Bas snapped. "The phone."

Jacob rubbed his hands up and down his arms, leaving one clasped over the wrapped tattoo. He'd had to do that himself this morning, for the first time since the night Bas had inked him. "Checking in with Josh," he said.

"How's your dad?"

"He's good."

With a curt nod, Bas turned his back and stepped to the other side of the block, shutting him out.

Jacob's stomach flipped again, landing ungracefully at his feet.

UNGRACEFUL BECAME A theme over the next two days.

Ungraceful starts, with Jacob off his timing and out of sorts as he hit the water. Ungraceful swims, as his mind drifted and his stroke suffered. Who would believe he'd been the one giving Terrence turn tips earlier in the week? Terrence, who continued to improve daily, who looked like a pro, while Jacob looked like he'd wandered in off the street, unsure what was going on.

Never more so than in medley relay practice. Jacob was used to focusing on Bas during his return lap, swimming harder to reach him, their breaths so in sync they didn't have to think about timing their exchange. They'd practiced that technique, back in Colorado and Texas, until it had become second nature. Now, however, after Bas's absence the last two nights and his cold shoulder in practices, Jacob was out of sync. His breathing was off, and he hesitated on his approach, uncertain who or what he was reaching for.

He wasn't handling Leah's advances gracefully either. And she was definitely making them—hanging out with him more at the pool, jogging by his side on morning runs, sitting with him at lunch. Jacob didn't mind the company; she was one of the bright spots in his increasingly gray days, her pleasant chatter filling the hours between practices and calls home. He wished he could return the favor, be a better friend and conversationalist.

With Bas out of reach, he'd started to think he might also like to be more than *just friends* with Leah, but between his mounting frustration and tendency to get tongue-tied, his uncoolness was a major stumbling block. One he didn't think even she could continue to ignore. He'd be lucky if she gave him the time of day once they reached Madrid. She'd be the one to find someone cooler and more interesting, then he'd lose his shot. Unless he channeled his cousin's swagger and made a move tonight.

Freshly determined, he turned his face toward the showerhead and pretended it could wash away the dork. He'd take a nap, watch an episode or two of *Black Sails*, and get his Charles Vane on. His determination wavered, however, when he heard the door to the room outside open and close.

If he had to guess, Bas would be in and out in a flash, just swinging by to grab his tablet. Jacob could hide in the bathroom and wait for him to leave again, or he could try to deal with some of the awkwardness now, before the team dinner. At minimum, he owed Bas an apology for the other night and for his shitty performance in the pool the past couple of days.

Toweling off quickly, he wrapped the terry cloth around his waist and stepped out of the bathroom, nearly running into Bas. As predicted, he was already on his way back out, tablet in hand. Path blocked, Bas stopped in his tracks, and the heat from his blue eyes raking over Jacob's torso scalded. And confounded. Jacob wasn't sure what he was seeing—or wasn't—anymore.

He cleared his throat, and Bas whipped his gaze to the

side, mumbling an apology. Jacob could have let it go, or made his own apology. Instead, eyes straying to Bas's perfectly made bed, Jacob lobbed a different question into the already murky waters between them.

"Where did you sleep last night?"

"Downstairs lounge." Bas brandished his tablet. "Fell asleep sketching."

"Oh." Perfectly reasonable, for a couple of hours, but none of the lounge couches were long enough for six-foot-plus Bas to sleep on all night.

"Night before that, I was at Ernie's," he added, unprompted.

Hearing Bas confirm Mike's rumor was a kick to Jacob's gut.

Bas's "on his couch" didn't soften the blow much either. He'd still chosen to sleep elsewhere, to continue to avoid him.

"You didn't have to do that," Jacob said.

"Violated the two-drink maximum," Bas replied. "Thought it safer to sober up first."

Jacob's eyes widened. "How much did you violate it by?"

Bas cupped a hand over his forehead, as if remembering the pain there. "A lot."

"So it's not just me the stress is getting to?"

Bas laughed, harsh and frustrated, yet it was still better than his silence. "You're not the only one. Not by a long shot." His eyes flickered up, exposing exhaustion. And not the satisfied sort.

Some of the pain in Jacob's gut eased, at the same time

worry for Bas bloomed. "I'll sleep in the lounge tonight," he offered.

"That's not necessary."

"You need to rest too. Sleep in your bed. If you need me gone, I'll be gone." The words tasted bitter, wrong, even though earlier he'd been hoping to be elsewhere, with Leah.

Bas's lips twisted, caught between a smile and a frown. "What about what you need?"

Jacob's breath caught and his mind stuttered, overloaded by too many answers to that very loaded question. Before he could grab hold of one, his phone rattled on the table, cutting off his deliberation. His nightly call from home was right on time. If he didn't answer it now, he wouldn't get another chance to talk to his dad tonight, and tomorrow was iffy, with traveling, opening ceremonies, and the Village opening-night party.

But would he get another chance to finish this conversation with Bas?

Torn, he glanced back and forth between the phone and Bas.

The latter made the decision for him, laying a hand on his shoulder and squeezing. "We'll work it out tonight, after dinner."

Jacob held Bas's hand there with one of his own. "You promise?"

"Promise. For now, go talk to your dad. Tell him I said hi."

For the first time in days, Jacob thought maybe he'd handled something gracefully.

CHAPTER
EIGHT

"SEBASTIAN, WAKE UP."

His full name, in Alex's captain-voice, roused Bas from sleep. Peeling his face off the wooden dining table, Bas stared up, into Alex's dark, assessing eyes.

"So this is where you're hiding now?"

The academy's high-ceilinged mess hall was as good a place as any. The dining area was mostly deserted until evening, and today, owing to their team dinner out, the kitchen staff were also absent. He'd had an hour to kill before they left for dinner, and he hadn't felt like socializing in the lounge or taking a walk outside in the ninety-degree heat. But he'd needed to get out of the room to give Jacob privacy and to save what was left of his good intentions.

The image of Jacob this afternoon, fresh from the shower, flashed behind his eyes again, and on its heels, blinding panic. For a split second, Bas feared his drawing of the memory, another reason he'd avoided the lounge, was displayed on his tablet screen for anyone to see. Including Alex.

A quick glance down and Bas sagged with relief. He'd

turned the device over, hiding today's sketch and the others. The one of Jacob's lust-wrecked face in the tattoo parlor mirror, every detail Bas could remember from that night etched into his digital likeness. The one of Jacob backed against the alley wall outside Martin's, eyes pleading and teeth digging into his full bottom lip. The one from today, Jacob's Longhorn tattoo the center of a profile sketch, water sluicing down his muscled torso and disappearing beneath the low-slung towel.

Yeah, he was hiding—too many things to count, the number growing by the day. "It's quiet in here," he claimed instead.

"You have a room to sleep in."

"Jacob was on the phone with his family. Wanted to give him some privacy."

Alex slid into the chair next to him. "That also why you slept in the lounge last night?"

Bas raised a brow, wanting to know who'd ratted him out.

"Kevin told me."

"Fell asleep sketching," Bas covered. "Everything's chill, Cap."

Alex braced his forearms on the table, glaring at him sideways. "I can't tell if you're too chill or less chill than I've ever seen you."

Maybe Bas shouldn't have answered at all. He hated lying to his best friend; he hated adding to his burdens more.

"I'm gonna go with the latter," Alex said when he didn't respond. "You want to tell me why?"

While he couldn't give Alex that truth, he could give him another—the truth about another wrong decision that'd been troubling him. "I fucked up with the Martin's idea." The team was jittery as hell, and the night out at Martin's had compounded their problems, not solved any.

"No, you didn't," Alex said. "If we hadn't gone out that night, the same breakdown would have happened after opening ceremonies instead. You were right. Like Coach said, better to get it out of our systems now."

Bas reclined in his chair, stretching out his legs and lacing his hands behind his head. "It seems worse than last time." And last time had been a fucking train wreck. "I didn't think that was possible."

"Me either." Alex's chuckle sounded more helpless than amused. "But this team's more talented. We didn't have the potential to win as many medals four years ago."

"You saying we're shining the spotlight brighter on ourselves?"

"That, plus the Ryan situation."

"And the Dane situation."

Alex leaned back, matching Bas's posture, his gaze drifting above to where his and Dane's room was. "There's something I need to tell you."

Alex's voice had gone tight, and some of Bas's earlier unease returned, now on behalf of his friend. "Is everything okay between you two? LA still on the table?"

"We're fine, and yes," Alex said, righting his gaze. "But we're likely to hit a speed bump next week. He's been ignoring his parents' calls."

"A lot of them?"

Alex cringed. "More than a few."

Dane's parents hadn't yet accepted that their golden goose had learned to use its wings and busted out of their conservative cage, taking all the sponsorship dollars with him. They'd thought his coming out as gay would cause Dane to lose sponsors, as well as tarnish the family's conservative reputation. In fact, he'd gained more sponsors, and Bas's mother, a high-powered LA attorney, was in the process of making sure only Dane's name was on those new contracts. And to hell with the family's reputation; maybe his parents' was tarnished, but Dane's was shining brighter than ever.

"They gonna cause trouble?" Bas asked.

"Likely," Alex replied. "They're en route to Madrid."

To force a confrontation, no doubt. Bas wished he was surprised, but from what he'd seen himself, and from what he'd heard from his mother, pushback was expected. He was more surprised they hadn't shown up already.

"Mom's gonna be in Madrid," Bas said. "I'll text her, put her on alert. We were expecting this. She'll be prepared."

"I know she will," Alex said, a smile turning up one corner of his mouth. "She's the scariest lawyer I know."

"She'd be pleased to hear it." Especially since she'd had to fight tooth and nail to get where she was today. Bas nudged his friend's shoulder. "Listen, Cap. No matter what, we've all got your backs. Both of you."

"Thank you," Alex said. "I'm glad we're both here again, that you're my second. Wouldn't want to do this with anybody else."

"And we're gonna do it this time. We're gonna win the gold."

Alex captured Bas's raised hand in a clasp. "Fuck yeah, we are."

CRAMMED TOGETHER AROUND long alfresco farm tables, the men's and women's swim teams helped themselves to platters of local delicacies and flasks of wine, drowning the past two days of rough practice in food and booze. A *heuriger*, the Viennese called it: a beer garden with wine, as far as Bas could tell. He liked the beer version better.

With travel tomorrow and opening ceremonies in the evening, the coaches had prebooked this last hoorah in their international training city. What was supposed to be a celebration was more a commiseration. Maybe that's what they needed. To not think about the past couple of days or the week ahead. Just enjoy this night, the here and now.

Sensing eyes on him, Bas lifted his gaze, eyes clashing with a pair of intense green ones at the far end of the table. Bas should look away, but he'd missed Jacob's regard and the connection between them. Flaring to life again, that connection simmered in Bas's chest, heating more as one corner of Jacob's mouth hitched. Bas had missed that smile too. But before it could bloom full, Coach Hartl stood at the head of his table and tapped his glass.

"I'm not gonna sugarcoat things," he said, once the chatter had quieted. "It's been a rough couple of days, but that's why we do international training. Get you used to being away—" he waved at the spread on the table in front of him "—and to the strange food."

"Come on, Coach," Sean said. "It's basically ham-and-cheese everything."

"Still can't pronounce it." Coach's struggles with German had been one of the few constant sources of amusement this week. "Good," Coach said over their laughter. "Ham it up, even if it is at my expense. That's what you fools need, because this only gets tougher from here. Opening ceremony tomorrow will be like nothing you've ever seen, but come Monday, you're in the pool against the best in the world."

"Not sure this is helping, Coach," Alex called out from beside Bas.

"Sure it is!" Coach Albert said, rising next to Hartl. "The rest of the world is gunning for us because they know we're the best." Her dark brown eyes swept the tables, lighting on each swimmer. "Aren't you? Who's the best?"

Fists on tables and chants of "U-S-A" rose up, starting at the coaches' table and spreading to the others, eventually loud enough for the entire hillside wine district to hear.

"That's right!" Hartl shouted. "You get this out of your systems. Have fun tonight and tomorrow, then we go to work. Let's win some medals!"

Cheers and toasts continued as teammates dug in to second helpings, the mood among them improving. Until Leah's raised voice echoed from the far end of the table.

"You're what?" Jacob's phone, in its burnt-orange case, slipped out of her hand and clattered onto the table. Leah recoiled from it, and Jacob, like she'd been bitten. "You're like the rest of them?"

Jacob turned fifteen shades of red as everyone's attention swung their direction. Leah's, however, shifted from Jacob, to Dane across the table, then to Bas and Alex.

"Fuck," Bas cursed. He had a pretty good idea what the anger was about, having been on the receiving end himself a time or ten.

He pushed to his feet, intending to intervene, but Alex grabbed his wrist, tugging him back down. "You'll only draw more attention. Dane's on it."

Beside Jacob, Big Red had leaned half across the table, a placating hand raised as he spoke too low to be overheard. After another minute, Jacob and Leah stood and moved their argument into the main winery building, the heavy wooden door banging shut behind them.

Straightening, Dane snatched up Jacob's phone and waved off the scene with his disarming smile. "Nothing to see here," he said. "And why aren't you fools eating?"

The spot-on impersonation of Coach drew raucous laughter and eased the tension that had fallen over the crowd. As the team tucked back into the meal, Dane strolled between the tables to where Alex was angled toward Bas. Stopping behind his boyfriend, Dane tapped the back of Alex's shoulder, ordering "Scoot."

Alex slid forward toward Bas, making enough room for Dane to straddle the bench behind him. "What the hell was that about?" Alex asked.

Dane snaked an arm around his waist, Jacob's phone faceup between the three of them. "Pup was showing her pictures of UT, and she swiped through to this one." Displayed on screen was a picture of Jacob kissing an attractive young man on the cheek. Playful, from a UT basketball game looked like, and definitely flirty. Bas swiped the screen. Texas to the left. More pictures of Jacob and the mystery man to the right.

"Boyfriend?" Bas asked, dreading the answer more than he should. Jacob had never mentioned anyone special back home, and surely if there had been someone, he would have visited when they were in San Antonio.

"Some guy he briefly dated last year," Dane answered.

"But?" Alex followed up, conveniently covering Bas's relieved sigh.

"Leah had no idea he was bi," Dane said. "Was none too happy about it."

Bas rewound to the first time he'd told a girl that Christian Bale was on his freebie-five list too. They hadn't dated much longer, and she hadn't been the last, of the men or women, who didn't get it. By the way Leah came storming back out of the winery, Bas guessed she didn't get it either. She bypassed her original seat and squeezed in with her girl posse at the other table, their heads diving together. A few whispered words from Leah, and they all turned to glare at Bas, Alex, and Dane.

"Fucking hell," Bas muttered, at the same time Alex ordered, "Damage control." Pocketing Jacob's phone, Bas stood, Alex right after him.

"I'll deal with Leah," Alex said. "You got Jacob?" Bas nodded and turned on his heel. "Keep me posted," Alex called behind him.

Charging inside the winery, Bas startled at the sudden blast of AC, a dramatic shift from the humid air outside. Rubbing his goose-bumped arms, he looked around for Jacob but didn't see his Chia Pet head anywhere. "Which way did the guy go?" he asked the host. "Tall, buzz cut, tattoo here," he said, tapping his upper arm where Jacob's ink peeked out from beneath his polo sleeve.

The host pointed toward the glass front door. "Down the hill toward town, I think."

Hurrying out, Bas was halfway down the hill before he spotted Jacob, the pup's rangy form disappearing around a shadowed street corner.

"Pup!" Bas cautiously hustled down the hill. Cobblestone was a recipe for broken bones, of which they'd had enough already. Jacob, however, didn't seem to care, moving at a faster clip. By the time Bas turned the same corner, Jacob was gone.

A car horn blared a street over.

Bas's thoughts careened toward his worst nightmares. Risking broken bones, he ran flat out to the end of the street and hung a left. Then nearly lost his dinner. Up ahead, Jacob wove unsteadily on the curb, arms flailing as he wiped angrily at his face. On these narrow streets, he was a side-view mirror away from a crushed hand, or an uneven stone away from far worse.

"Jacob!" he hollered, heart in his throat.

The younger man startled, his unbalanced turn setting off another chorus of car horns. Bas didn't think, just acted. Darting forward, he wrapped an arm around Jacob's waist and hauled him back.

Spitting mad, Jacob struggled in his hold. "Let go of me!"

"Hey now." Bas dragged him into a covered shop entry and held him pressed against the darkened storefront. "Enough of that."

"It's always the same fucking thing."

"What is?"

Jacob lifted his arms, as if to rail, then suddenly deflated, letting them collapse at his sides. "I mean, I haven't been out that long, just a couple years, but I've always known. I didn't think it'd be this hard, though. That it would doom me to dating hell, not that I wasn't there already. They just don't get it."

Another page to Jacob's story. One Bas knew the words to by rote, from his own miserable love life. He brushed his thumbs through the tear tracks on Jacob's cheeks. "I know."

"It's not an either-or thing. It's men *and* women," Jacob said, blinking rapidly as more tears threatened.

"Jacob, I know," Bas repeated. "I've been there. I've heard it from men and women too. Let me guess what she said. 'You're checking out the guys too?' And I'm sure you've also heard, 'So I have to compete with twice as many people for your attention?'"

"Like it's some sort of fucking percentage. And the denominator isn't even right when you include nonbinary and transgender people." Jacob angrily wiped at his running nose, then dropped his head back against the storefront glass, a watery chuckle escaping. "God, I'm never gonna get laid at this rate."

A barrage of images assaulted Bas, foremost of which was where that night in the tattoo parlor might have led to if he'd pushed. He hadn't then, and he couldn't now, no matter how tempting. "You're only nineteen, Pup."

"And still a virgin."

"That's not a bad thing."

Jacob righted his head and his tired eyes looked closer to forty than twenty. "It is when it's another thing added to the mountain of *not good enough*. Something else the dorky *kid* can't do right, on top of a shit week. Dad has a flashback. I fuck up at Martin's, and you freeze me out." Bas winced, but Jacob didn't notice. "I suck in the pool. You can say it doesn't matter, that it's all fine, but it's not. Hell, Terrence should be swimming with you guys, not me."

"That's something else we need to talk about," Bas started, but Jacob rambled right over him.

"I just wanted to forget all of it, for one night. Before we got to Madrid and Leah realized how not cool I am. This was my last shot."

Christ, did he have no idea what he was doing to Bas? Standing this close, this vulnerable, this beautiful, and offering up everything Bas had wanted the past three and a half weeks. But Bas couldn't—*wouldn't*—take advantage. Not when Jacob was this upset, and not when it was Leah on the pup's mind. It was her affection—not Bas's—he'd wanted. As much as it burned Bas's gut, Leah was a safer bet for Jacob, *if* she came around. She didn't have *deserter* stamped on her DNA like Bas did. He stepped back, out of Jacob's space. "I can go talk to her," he offered. "See if I can explain things."

Jacob shot out a hand, grasping the front of Bas's shirt and halting his retreat. "No," he said, voice small yet sure. "We shouldn't have to explain."

No, they shouldn't.

Bas did the only thing he could. He hauled Jacob in and held him tight. "You're right," he mumbled against the top of his head. "You shouldn't have to explain or change, for anyone."

Hands fisting in Bas's shirt, Jacob finally let the sobs loose, his shoulders hitching as the dam broke. Face buried in his chest, Jacob hid from the world, seeking refuge in Bas's arms.

Bas gladly provided it, cradling Jacob's head and rubbing his other hand over Jacob's back. "Let it out, Pup. It's all right. I've got you."

Like this, Bas would give him anything. Everything.

CHAPTER
NINE

WRAPPED IN BAS'S arms in the back seat of a cab, his senses flooded with everything Sebastian, Jacob made his decision. Stupid, awkward, and likely a long shot, but Bas understood what Leah didn't, what Emily and Wes hadn't. Bas had said it was all right. That Jacob didn't have to change. That he had him. Jacob had asked Bas to stay before and he had—back in San Antonio. He'd be asking more now. Jacob prayed the answer would be different than after Martin's the other night.

Bas's hand on his back as they exited the cab was a shot of confidence. As was Bas standing close as they claimed their room keys from security, and Bas, hand still on his back, leading him past the lounge to their room, on the same side of the closed door for the first time in two nights.

In the short entry hall, Bas stepped past him, reaching for the light, and Jacob acted on his decision. His maneuvers, when focused, in the water or in combat, were far from awkward. Using one of the martial arts moves his father had taught him, Jacob caught Bas's raised wrist and spun him around, slamming his back against the wall. Holding his outstretched arm against the wall, Jacob curled his other hand around Bas's neck.

"Jacob," Bas gasped, lifting his free hand between them.

Had he said *Pup*, Jacob might have stopped. But Bas didn't. So neither did Jacob. He slanted his mouth over Bas's, crashing his lips against the ones he'd barely brushed the other night and had wanted every second since. They were warm from the outside, chapped from the chlorine . . . and unmoving.

As was the man he held pinned.

Fuck.

Had he read this wrong again?

Ready to walk the plank of mortification once more and claim that underwater locker, Jacob pulled back to gauge Bas's anger. Only it wasn't anger he saw. Bas's blown-wide pupils blotted out his blue irises and a deep blush stained his high cheekbones. Add to that the pounding pulse beneath Jacob's hand, and the stiffening cock against his thigh, and Jacob didn't think he'd read this wrong after all.

Parting his lips, Bas ran his tongue along where Jacob's lips had been pressed.

Jacob watched, enraptured, his own cock aching. "Please, Bas," he whispered. "I just want somebody to fuck me. For one night."

Bas inhaled sharply and retreated as much as the wall would allow. "'Somebody'?"

"*You.*" Releasing Bas's wrist, Jacob trailed his hand slowly up Bas's arm, tracing the colorful designs. "I watched you on TV four years ago, and I thought you were the most gorgeous being I'd ever seen. And then I met you at Trials, and you were even more gorgeous in person."

The hand against Jacob's chest pushed him away. "So this is some kind of fan fantasy?" Bas's clipped tone sent Jacob reeling back another step.

"Yes," he said, trying to pay a compliment, then brain catching up to his mouth, corrected his stalker-ific mistake. "I mean no!"

Shit, he was screwing this up. Raking a hand over his head, cursing again his hair that was no longer there to grab, he took a deep breath and started over.

"I know you now. You get me. But yes," he admitted, because fuck, it was out there already, "I've fantasized about you, for years."

Bas growled, the good kind, and the sound went straight to Jacob's dick. Lifting his hands, he approached slowly and laid his palms on Bas's chest, running them over the hard, toned muscles beneath the cotton polo. "It was you I was thinking about that night in the tattoo parlor."

Eyes flashing, Bas grabbed him by the shirt and yanked him closer. "I am not a fantasy."

"I know." Jacob rubbed against him, from chest to cock. "I want the real thing, not the fantasy."

"What about Leah?"

"You're the one who gets me. I want you."

In the blink of an eye, Bas forced them across the foyer, and Jacob's back hit the opposite wall. Despite the strength unleashed, the hands that rose to cradle his face were gentle.

As gentle as anyone had been with him in years.

"Are you sure?" Bas asked.

"Stay tonight, please."

Bas answered with a deep groan and a breath-stealing kiss. Fierce and gentle at the same time, Bas drove his tongue through Jacob's lips, plundering his mouth, as he cushioned Jacob's head from the wall with his hands. With a thigh shoved between his legs, crushing the rest of him between a hard body and cool plaster, Jacob hummed contentedly as Bas pinned him. Face caged between colorful arms, body warmly trapped, he was safe in the cocoon of Bas's creation, the other man always looking out for him, even in this.

But the cocoon wasn't quite complete. Snaking his arms around Bas's neck, Jacob reached up and blindly unwound the rubber band holding together Bas's topknot. Loosened, long blond dreads tumbled around them. Jacob had seen them down so seldom, he took a second to admire, but only just, as Bas's mouth coasted lower, lips and tongue teasing his throat.

The strangled "ungh" he made was humiliating, but Bas's deep chuckle in the crook of his neck wiped the embarrassment clean. Jacob had missed that sound. Head lolling to the side, gaze snagging on Bas's arm, Jacob eyed the tattoos he so badly wanted to touch. And taste. He tugged at the back of Bas's shirt, trying to get it off.

Bas stepped out of his arms, and the cocoon shattered.

The rising panic—that this was all just a dream, that Bas would change his mind, that Jacob had asked too much and would be left alone again—must have shown on his face. Bas finished yanking off the shirt and rushed close, framing his face. "Hey now," he whispered. "I'm right here." Bas kissed him, unhurried and deep, and Jacob's panic receded, reassured of the here and now. When next they broke, it was Jacob who wandered south, trailing his mouth down Bas's neck to the top of his right shoulder where the tattoos started.

Jacob's fingers led, touching; his lips followed, tasting.

The dark line work brought to mind licorice, chocolate, and the Turkish coffee Bas loved so much.

The reds and purples, summer berries.

Yellows, sun and sweat.

The blues and greens, water and chlorine—neither a figment of his imagination like the others, the hours they spent in the pool impossible to wash away.

Their lower bodies began to rock, finding a rhythm as Jacob continued his exploration, torturing them both with fingers and lips. Until he neared the lonely initials on Bas's chest. Bas cut off his tour, hauling him up, and Jacob feared he'd done something wrong.

Bas silenced his doubts with another claiming kiss. A noise escaped, another mortifying "ungh," when Bas slid a hand down between them and palmed Jacob's cock through his jeans, stroking him up and down. Jacob was lucky he didn't come right then.

Bas snickered against his lips. "Think you're ready for bed."

Jacob nodded furiously but couldn't reason how to move off the wall. Bas, of sounder mind and body, peeled him from the plaster and led him into the room, hand at his lower back. They shuffled to the side of Jacob's bed, where Bas left him with a gruff, "Undress."

Shedding his clothes, Jacob was suddenly struck shy, which was ridiculous since he and Bas had shared a room and countless locker room showers. But everything about this moment was different—the intent, where it might lead, what it might mean. He kicked his jeans and boxers aside as doubt resurfaced. Was he really going to do this? Live out his fantasy? Risk the morning, the team, the medley relay gold for one night for himself? And what if this one night went horribly? What if he embarrassed himself more? Handjobs and blowjobs were one thing, but Bas was experienced, and he was still—

A bottle of lube hit the bed, and Jacob gulped back his runaway doubts. He was sure Bas heard them. "Gonna ask one more time. You sure, Pup?"

Fifty-fifty, but when rough hands landed on his hips and a hard cock nestled against his ass, uncertainty fled, burned away by raging desire. Seizing Bas's left hand, Jacob drew it down to his cock. "Yeah," he panted, thrusting into Bas's grip. "I'm sure." He angled his face, kissing the underside of Bas's prickly jaw. "We need condoms."

"Not the only way to fuck."

Jacob only had a second to be disappointed before Bas dipped his head and captured his lips, all gentleness gone. Tongue plunging into Jacob's mouth, hand stroking his cock, Bas rocked against his backside and shuffled them forward. When his shins hit the mattress, Jacob climbed up on the bed, Bas following behind him, never once letting go of his mouth or cock. They stroked, rocked, and kissed until Bas broke away, nuzzling the spot behind Jacob's ear. "Grab the bottle."

Bending, Jacob reached for the lube, and Bas's hand coasted over his backside, fingers tantalizingly close to where Jacob wanted them most. He fumbled the bottle but came up with it on the second try. The hand on his backside disappeared, then reappeared in front of him, palm up. "Pour it," Bas ordered.

Hands shaking, Jacob managed to snap the lid open and up-end the bottle, squeezing a generous amount into Bas's palm. Jacob thought he was going to use it on his cock, but Bas began to jack himself instead.

Jacob nearly shot. "I want to do it," he begged, starting to turn.

Bas had other ideas, slapping Jacob's hip with his other hand. "Legs in a little tighter."

Confused but willing to follow Bas anywhere, Jacob did as told, and promptly had his mind and world blown. Bas's slick cock eased between his thighs, rubbing across his taint and nudging the backs of his balls.

"Oh God," Jacob groaned, head falling back onto Bas's shoulder. Slick hand reaching around, Bas jerked him off, drawing out more incomprehensible sounds, until he claimed another deep, devouring kiss, dreads falling all around them.

Rough and gentle.

Everything of Jacob's fantasies.

"Not gonna last," he panted when they came up for air.

"You don't have to last. Lean forward and grab the headboard." Bas splayed a hand in the middle of his back. "Ride it, Jacob. Ride my cock, and let go."

Words were too hard. The pressure in his balls was too hard. His cock was beyond too hard, bordering on painful. He tightened his thighs and bore down, loving it when Bas rocked harder. Switching hands, Bas jacked him faster, while his slick fingers trailed over Jacob's ass and down his crack, teasing his rim. Jacob's muscles clenched, trying to draw him in, and his cock exploded, come filling Bas's hand and dripping through his fingers onto the sheets. Bas grunted behind him, thrusting until a surge of hot, sticky wetness coated Jacob's thighs.

Under their combined weight, Jacob sank to the bed, taking Bas with him. He ignored the mess and enjoyed the warm weight of Bas half on top of him, lulling him to sleep with soothing passes of his hand over his back. "That's it, Pup. I've got you."

He turned his head toward Bas and smiled unseeing, losing the battle with his eyelids. "Jacob," he said. "I like when you call me Jacob."

Bas's hand swept from his shoulder, down his back, and over his ass. Jacob tried to give chase, to lift his hips after it, but he was so tired. Had been for days. But he was safe now, here with Bas; he could rest.

Bas's lips brushed over his. "Sleep, Jacob."

"Only if you stay," he mumbled half to the pillow, half to Bas.

He was asleep by the time Bas answered.

JACOB SHIFTED ON the bed and winced, the sheets sticking to his chest and stomach, an uncomfortable reminder of the previous night's pleasant activities. And a reminder he needed to shave soon, now that the meet was finally upon them. He smiled into his pillow, eager for the day ahead, for a change. Until a blast of cold air hit his back and his groggy mind woke the rest of the way up, realizing what—*who*—was missing. No soothing hand coasting over his back, no warm body blanketing him, no blond dreadlocks sweeping his shoulders.

Eyes still closed, he rolled off his stomach and peeled away the sheets, hoping against hope, and the realities of a twin bed, that maybe Bas was still in it with him. His bare back hit cool plaster and hope faded.

No Bas.

Just Jacob.

Cold and alone.

This was why he never asked for what he wanted, never put himself first. The opposite invariably resulted.

He yanked the sheet up over his head, not wanting to face the cold, disappointing morning. Bas was gone or asleep in the other bed, having left Jacob's. Either option shattered the fantasy cocoon he'd inhabited last night. He'd been spiraling, on his way to hitting rock bottom, but Bas had caught him, wrapped him up safe and sound, and given him what he'd asked for.

Well, most of it.

Not the only way to fuck, Bas had said, and proved it. Jacob had fallen asleep satisfied, disappointment banished. But in the lonely light of morning, he was second-guessing everything. Had Bas even wanted to fuck him? Jacob had thought so, by the way Bas had hungrily kissed him, how he'd taken care of him, by the groan and shudder of Bas's body behind him when they'd come.

But was all that just a favor for Jacob? Was Jacob so terrible in bed that Bas had fled? Or had it really meant nothing to Bas? Just some handjobs, simulated fucking, and a little ass play? Had Bas ever intended to stay? Realizing he'd fallen asleep before hearing Bas's answer, never hearing a yes, sent Jacob spiraling again.

His blaring phone alarm greeted him at the bottom.

No curses or groans from across the room.

Bas was definitely gone, then.

Jacob opened his eyes, verifying what the rest of his senses had told him. Adding insult to injury, Bas's bags were packed and on his bed. He'd done all that while Jacob slept, then left. A third morning waking up alone.

Scooting off the end of the bed, Jacob snagged his pants, dug out his phone, and silenced the alarm. Device in hand, he ignored the low-battery warning and scrolled through his other notifications—no messages from Bas. He considered texting him, then decided against it, not wanting to confirm his failure just yet.

He plugged the phone into the wall charger, grabbed his

undergarments, and carried them into the bathroom. He startled at his reflection in the mirror. His body didn't look like it'd been used by someone who didn't care. With a careful hand, he tested the tenderness of the kiss bruises on his neck, compared his fingers to the marks left by longer ones on his hips, and stared at the bruises on the backs of his thighs.

Thank God they were in suits today, and thank God for jammers, because he looked like he'd been fucked by someone who'd wanted him badly. Hope flickered as he washed away the other evidence of last night's desire on his thighs and stomach. Maybe Bas had gone for a run, or downstairs to the lounge to sketch, or out to grab a couple of coffees for them. Maybe the worst case Jacob's mind had jumped to wasn't the case at all.

He hurried through the rest of his shower, toweled off, and tugged on his boxers and undershirt. When he stepped back into the room, Bas was there, tucking his tablet into his messenger bag. But unlike yesterday, when Bas had seemed withdrawn and surly, today he was smiling wide. In his light gray suit, pristine white shirt, and blue paisley tie, eyes glowing to match and dreads tied neatly back, he looked stunning.

Jacob crossed to stand behind him. "Hi."

Bas glanced over his shoulder, and his smile faltered. "Hi."

"You left early," Jacob said, ignoring the creeping tendrils of doubt trying to snuff out his wavering hope. "I didn't hear you shower."

Bas zipped up his bag. "Alex and Dane's room."

Stepping closer, Jacob considered running his hands over Bas's shoulders and down his arms, but the stiff set of the other man's spine warned against it. Jacob's hands hung suspended in midair, before he lowered them. "You didn't have to do that."

Bas slipped out from in front of him, the split of his suit coat whispering over Jacob's fingertips. "I didn't want to wake you."

As Bas moved around his bed, checking closets and drawers for stray items, Jacob retreated to his side of the room and dressed. Doubt no longer crept; it stomped with each fluttering beat of Jacob's sinking heart. "How are they this morning?" he asked, struggling to make conversation.

"Alex and Dane? Good. Mo called." Dane's mentor, and a close friend of Alex and Bas, Mo had made the team but not the trip, sidelined by an injury back in Colorado Springs. "His wife had the twins."

That explained Bas's earlier smile. "Why didn't you say so? Or come wake me so I could have been there with you?"

"You hardly knew Mo."

Jacob staggered where he stood, shirt half buttoned, tie hanging loose around his neck. "I did know Mo. He's a teammate." Such a momentous occasion in any teammate's life meant something to all of them. Or did Bas not think Jacob a true member of the team? He was just the new guy, one who performed erratically at best. He could be replaced. Alex and Dane had a history, Alex and Bas were best friends. They'd closed ranks around their family, leaving him on the outside, alone.

He grabbed his father's dog tags and sank onto the end of his bed, staring down as he tumbled the metal plates. "I would have liked to have been there."

Bas's big hand covered his, stilling the motion, and when Jacob looked up, Bas was kneeling in front of him, face and voice no longer cold, but not inviting either. "You needed the sleep, Pup."

"I needed—"

Bas's fingers tightened. "One night, that's what you said you needed."

Yes, that was what he'd said, all he'd asked for, and by the flash of something across Bas's eyes—a plea almost—one night was all Bas could give. Jacob had known that in his head, but his heart . . . He was fourteen all over again, asking for more than he could or should. Jacob glanced away, before he asked Bas to stay and sent him packing for good.

"Now, we need to work." Standing, Bas grabbed his bags and headed for the door. "Bus leaves in ten. Alex wants to talk media strategy, and Dane has some pointers. We'll save you a seat."

Jacob tried to convince himself it was all he needed. Bas was still talking to him, Alex still considered him a teammate, and Dane thought enough of him to give him pointers. But as the dog tags slipped from his grasp and hit the floor, the sound as hollow as he felt, Jacob knew he needed more.

CHAPTER
TEN

ULTRAMODERN IN DESIGN, with sharp angles, big windows, and gleaming exterior walls, Madrid's Olympic Village was bright. Every surface reflected the afternoon sun, blinding Bas—supremely unhelpful as he, Alex, Nat, and Eva herded their teams along the crowded promenade toward resident check-in. Supremely unhelpful too were the many interruptions along the way. While Bas enjoyed seeing some of the returning athletes, friends he'd stayed in touch with on social media and at smaller meets, he did not relish the leering ones who approached with proposition after proposition. He'd made a name for himself at the last Olympics, not a good one, and the reminders of his mistakes were everywhere. By some grace of the deity, the biggest one was not here yet, but Jacob, following behind Bas, had a front-row seat to the rest.

The pup had started to hang back after the tenth or so hookup offer, keeping himself apart from Bas and the team. Wonder shone in his big green eyes, but so did hurt and uncertainty. After the incident at the *heuriger*, rumors had swirled about Jacob's sexuality and whether he'd intentionally kept the truth from Leah. Given the way she'd reacted, would anyone blame him if he had? Which Bas doubted, regardless. Jacob had more likely kept his bisexuality quiet to avoid creating drama. The fact that it'd backfired, and he was now the center of attention, was no doubt eating him alive.

That's not what the team needs, he'd said, together with a litany of apologies, as they'd discussed media strategy with Alex and Dane on the way here.

Last night, Bas had meant to give Jacob what he'd needed, putting Leah, the team, and all of it aside for one night and writing a different page in the pup's story, one where Jacob wasn't always the giver. But Bas had taken too much for himself instead. So this morning he'd put some distance between them. Not as much as after Martin's—he'd still be there for Jacob as a mentor—but Bas wouldn't let it go further. Because if he allowed himself more, he'd take and take, and then when nothing was left, he'd leave, like he'd done before, like he was bound to do again. Jacob didn't deserve or need that.

"I still can't believe Jacob's a player," Leah said, close behind Bas, jarring him out of his thoughts. "I didn't think he was like that."

Bas wanted to turn and rail, the misconceptions in Leah's statement, her completely wrong reading of Jacob, making his blood boil. Jacob was right. They shouldn't have to explain any of this to her, to anyone, but they needed to address this sooner rather than later for the sake of the team. And better him than Jacob.

Channeling Alex's calm, he slowed his stride and waited

for the group of women to catch up.

"Hey, Leah," he said. "You got a minute?"

She tried to skirt around him. "We're late for check-in."

He blocked her path, hands up. He didn't want to pressure, but clearly whatever Alex had said to her last night hadn't penetrated. "It'll just take a minute," he said.

"Go on, Leah," Natalie said, joining them. "Hear Bas out."

Leah looked back and forth between them, ultimately listening to her captain. "Sure, okay."

Bas led Leah off the walkway, out of the sea of slow-moving people and onto the grass near one of the man-made ponds. "Last week in Vienna," he started, "you and Jacob were hanging out a lot."

"Yeah, so." Leah carded her fingers through her short brown hair.

"What'd you like about hanging out with him?"

"What are you getting at?"

"Humor me."

She shrugged one shoulder. "He's a really good swimmer, I guess."

Bas pressed. "That much time together, it must have been about more than race tips."

"We like a lot of the same stuff." She glanced at him through her lashes, reluctant at first, then growing more animated as she spoke. "TV shows, books, sports. He's a total dork, but it's cute. And he makes me laugh. He's real, you know?"

"And *he's* cute." Her eyes grew round, and Bas grinned,

cutting through more of the tension. "Hey, just calling it like I see it."

"Yeah, he is," she admitted with her own small smile.

"And does any of that stuff you like about Jacob change because he's bisexual?" He waited for the realization to sink in, Leah's cheeks heating when it did. "Who Jacob loves doesn't change any of that. It's just another part of who he is, and that's the same adorkable Jacob you hung out with all last week."

Leah lowered her chin, suddenly interested in her shoes.

"And being bisexual doesn't make him a player. To tell the truth, I don't think Jacob could pull off *player* if he tried."

"I was surprised, is all."

"Don't make assumptions and you're less likely to be surprised." It was a common mistake, assuming a hetero default for everyone. Bas had gotten used to it; didn't make it any less annoying.

"I've never known anyone who was bi before."

"That you know of."

She lifted her chin, lips tipping up in a smile again. "Hashtag facepalm."

Bas could see why Jacob liked her—their senses of humor aligned. "You have any questions, ask me. Or Jacob. Give him a chance, okay? Jacob likes you, and you're pretty cool about most things; be cool about this too."

"I'm sorry."

He jutted his chin toward Jacob, who was walking up ahead with Terrence. "Tell him that."

She promised to do so, apologized again, and rushed off to join Nat and the rest of the women's team near the front of the check-in line. He turned to rejoin the guys and nearly ran into Sean and Kevin, the team gossips, eavesdropping.

Bas rolled his eyes. "You two overheard that?"

"We didn't mean to," Sean lied.

"We were just talking about video games," Kevin added.

"And listening." He waved a finger between them. "You Golden Girls forget I know your routine." They didn't deny it or the moniker. "Either of you got issues with Jacob we need to address?" He had to ask, given Kevin's somewhat obtuse reaction to Dane's coming out. He'd been cool since, but, for what Bas was contemplating, Kevin needed to be cool with Jacob too.

"Nah, man," Sean answered. "Pup's a good kid."

"No problem here," Kevin echoed.

"Good, he's the third in your triple." Bas had seen the room assignments on Alex's desk this morning. They technically hadn't filled the third spot—didn't need to—but Bas was making an executive decision.

Kevin didn't seem to like it. "Shit, for real?"

"I thought you didn't have a problem with Jacob."

"I don't. It's the crowded triple I got a problem with." He waggled his brows. "All so *you* can have a shag pad to yourself."

Bas remained silent, letting him believe that was the reason.

Sean backed his play. "We can do our man a solid." He shoved Kevin's shoulder, grin full of mischief. "And now ours will be the party room."

Then again, maybe re-rooming Jacob with them *wasn't* the smartest idea if Sean and Kevin were going to be off the hook. From what Bas could remember, they'd been relatively well behaved last time around. That said, he hadn't been paying close attention, distracted as he was.

They split before Bas could change his mind, corralling Jacob from Terrence and sliding their arms over his shoulders. Maybe *not* a bad idea, except for the fact they almost took Jacob down with their enthusiasm. Or did Jacob's stumble, as he glanced back over his shoulder at Bas, have more to do with the flash of betrayal in his eyes and the deflated slump of his shoulders?

Coward that he was, Bas gave an encouraging nod that he didn't feel and looked away, searching for Alex. He spotted Dane first, his bright red mop above the rest, then Alex's dark one beside him. Bas hustled their direction and shoved in line next to them.

"What's up?" Alex said.

"Put Jacob in the triple with Sean and Kevin."

Alex raised a brow.

"After that shit with Leah, the rest of the team needs to see he's not just hanging out with the queer guys."

"And you?" Dane said. The poster boy was smarter than he looked.

Bas ignored him and the implication. "Put someone else with me if you need to."

"We're square," Alex said, but not without a serious side-eye. "Something more to that room reassignment?"

"Just doing what's best for the team," Bas answered, hoping like hell Alex bought it. And hoping like hell this was the best thing for Jacob too.

"LIKE NOTHING YOU'VE EVER SEEN."

Coach was right about the Olympic Opening Ceremony.

Jacob thought he'd seen pomp and circumstance before—the lengths Texans would go for football games were legendary—but nothing he'd seen back home compared to this.

Marching into Olympic Stadium with the rest of Team USA, Jacob made no attempt to hide his wonder. He struggled with where to look; he wanted to see it all, but there was so much. *Sensory overload* wasn't a strong enough descriptor for the assault of sights and sounds competing for his attention. The roof overhang with its undulating spoke structure that seemed to move with the wavelike projections of the Olympic colors. The stands, three levels high, jam-packed with spectators and press. The lighted inner-oval stage overflowing with dancers and performers. And all around Jacob on the track, athletes from other countries dressed in their teams' distinctive outfits. *Outfits* was likewise not the right word, but neither was *costumes*. Each country's culture was unique and shone through in their athletes' attire. Jacob wanted to run up to each new team he passed and ask why that hat, or why that pattern, so much of it new and different to him.

"Pup!" Alex shouted. He was waving his arms, flagging Jacob forward. "Get up here."

Shuffling through the crowd, Jacob noticed the rest of his teammates, even the Olympic vets, were likewise awestruck, making him feel less like a noob. When he reached Alex, and Bas by his side, Jacob kept his smile in place, forcing himself not to dwell on the unexpected room reassignment earlier that afternoon. Not here, not now. He would enjoy this moment and worry about the other later.

"Surprise for you," Alex said, grabbing him by the wrist and dragging him forward. Bas cut a path for them, and before Jacob knew what was happening, they were at the front of Team USA and the basketball player Jacob had idolized most of his life was handing him the US flag.

Smiling wide, still half in a starstruck daze, Jacob wrapped his hands around the pole and carried the flag for the next quarter of a lap, sweat trickling down his back under the designer dress shirt and jacket. It was worth it to carry his country's flag, to feel a part of Team USA, and to give his friends and family back home a thrill. Jacob let the happiness and wonder carry him away for a while. The music, fireworks, and spectacle—and his teammates' excitement—were magical. He'd been training hard for weeks, years, and tonight it really hit him what it was all for. To swim for Team USA at the Olympics. It was terrifying and exhilarating all at once.

The craziness didn't stop after their lap around the stadium. Once they stepped off the track and back inside the building, the full-court press was on, literally. Press, agents, and sponsors shouted from all directions, and Bas had been right. There were questions for Alex and Dane, but just as many directed at him.

"What's it feel like to be a first-time Olympian?"

"Amazing," Jacob answered. "And a huge responsibility."

"Is medley relay going to win gold?"

"That's our plan," Dane answered beside him.

"Did you know you'd get to carry the flag, Jacob?"

"No, that was a surprise."

"Was that the best part of the night?"

"Absolutely!"

"And the worst?"

He tugged at his collar. "These outfits are freaking hot. I love the colors and the design. Very Team USA." He swept a hand down, Vanna White-like. "But did no one tell the designer it'd be ninety degrees here?"

The reporters tittered, while Dane laughed. "Well, there goes that sponsorship."

Jacob gulped and looked over his shoulder. "I shouldn't have said that?"

Dane grinned and tugged open his own collar, putting Jacob at ease. "Nah, you just said what we're all thinking. Don't worry about it, kid."

Once the ceremonies and unofficial Q&A were over, they returned to Olympic Village, which was humming with first-night parties. The adrenaline should have kept Jacob going, but as soon as he stood next to his bed in the triple, his excitement waned, the second-guessing he'd pushed aside earlier rearing its head. Sharing a room with Bas would have been awkward, Jacob knew that. Still, it'd been a surprise when Kevin and Sean had given him the news. Bas had confirmed it with a nod, and Jacob had turned away quickly, hiding the fall of his face. Madly dashing to register, peeing in a cup for the drug tests, changing into their opening-ceremony attire, and getting in line for the processional had distracted him, and then the ceremony itself had buoyed him. But now, it was like this morning all over again. He'd been separated from his mentor, his closest friends on the team, and his medley relay squad.

"Pup," Sean said, strolling out of the attached bathroom. "You look like you lost your pup."

Jacob cleared his throat, giving as bland an answer as possible. "Sorry, just a little homesick." He didn't want Sean and Kevin to think he wasn't happy to room with them. They'd been great actually, not making a big deal out of the Leah situation or the last-minute room reassignment. They were taking the switch up in stride, and Jacob was glad not to be a burden.

"Dude," Kevin said from his corner of the room. "No time for homesickness. We gotta party. This is our last night off."

"For you maybe," Sean said. "Some of us have races tomorrow." He was first up in the four-hundred-meter free.

"And heats," Jacob added. His hundred-meter breast-stroke heat was in the morning.

Kevin waved them off. "You're both ready. Come on. I gotta scout out the condom fishbowls. Find the best."

Sean splayed his fingers. "I spotted five in the lounge."

"Good," Kevin said, puffing out his chest "Because those Aussie swimmers . . ." He trailed off, whistling low. "Though I know you've got your eye on Natalie," he said with a wink at Sean.

Ignoring him, Sean elbowed Jacob's side. "See any you like, Pup?"

Yeah, the big, tall one with blond dreadlocks and tattoos who'd kissed and fucked him senseless, but that had only been for one night.

Kevin pushed Sean aside and stood directly in front of Jacob, clutching his shoulders and giving him a shake. "Okay, listen, you're new at this. Sean and I have been here before, so rule number one, the most important rule: we will not be the mopey room. I forbid it."

Jacob raised a brow. "You forbid it?"

"Aye, Pup," he replied in a poor, but valiant, imitation of Jacob's favorite accent. "That's yes for pirate speak, right?"

Jacob couldn't help but smile. "Aye, matey, now where's this party you speak of?"

"There he is!" Sean cheered, as Kevin clapped his shoulders.

A half hour later, changed into jeans and a Team USA polo, Jacob headed downstairs with his roommates to the building's lounge. He halted over the threshold, mouth agape. This was nothing like their TV marathons in Vienna or San Antonio, where the team had sprawled across couches, relaxed and comfy in wrinkled athletic wear. This was closer to a rave, or a frat party with a bunch of hot, decked-out athletes. All of the furniture had been pushed against the walls, Euro pop of some techno variety was cranked loud, and a crowd danced in the center of the large room.

"Does it stay like this the whole time?" Jacob asked.

"Pretty much," Sean said. "Though the crowd makeup depends on the sport. This is the last night us swimmers have off. We're competing the first week. So after tonight, we shut down and the track and basketball guys—" he pointed at the giants in the far corner, including the baller who'd handed Jacob the flag "—keep the party going until we rejoin the festivities at the end of the week. Oh, there's Nat!"

Sean took off after Natalie, and Kevin braved the crowd, eyes locked on an attractive leggy blond. Jacob diverted to the drink table instead, grabbing a bottle of water. On the other end of the table sat one of the infamous bowls of condoms, of which he'd be needing none. His good mood darkened, then wobbled precariously close to black when Leah tapped his shoulder.

"Oh, hi," he said cautiously.

"Can we talk for a minute?" She tilted her head toward a less crowded corner of the room, and Jacob followed. "I owe you an apology," she said, once they were far enough removed from the others. "I'm sorry."

Jacob was surprised; he'd expected a barrage of questions or leftover animosity, certainly not an apology.

"Hey, you didn't know any better," he said, waving it off, as he usually did. He didn't want to make anyone feel awkward. It was rare enough he ever got an apology. "I'm sorry I surprised you."

She shook her head. "No, I shouldn't have assumed. Bas made me see that."

"Bas?"

"He explained the bi thing to me. You're still you, and I like you." She stepped closer, her flirtatious smile and interested eyes revived. "I think he's playing matchmaker."

Jacob's improving mood cratered. If Bas was setting him up with Leah, then any romantic shot he had with Bas was officially off the table. One night was all Bas could give; Jacob would have to accept that. But he didn't want to throw himself into something with Leah either, not while he still had a shred of hopeless, ill-advised desire for Bas. And not while he still didn't totally trust her. No one needed more team drama, and Jacob didn't want to be the cause of it. "I think maybe just friends, if that's okay with you?"

Her smile dimmed a little, but then she resurrected the bright one and looped an arm through his. "I'd like that. You're funny and cool."

"You know, you're the first person who's ever called me cool."

She swatted at his head, setting off a debate as to who was cooler in their dorky uncoolness. After a few minutes, Leah leaned closer. "Don't look now, but your uncoolness has caught the eye of the hottest guy here."

He looked up, expecting blond dreadlocks and painted skin, but Bas was nowhere to be seen. And of course Bas hadn't been who Leah was referring to. Taken generally, most of the guys here were hot. "Now you're playing matchmaker?"

"It's kind of fun when I have even more people to work with." She gestured at the crowd parting to their left. "Hottie incoming."

She wasn't wrong. Tall, dark, and handsome was heading straight for them, eyes on Jacob. The guy looked a few years older than him, but was otherwise the same height and build. Jacob would bet money on him being a swimmer, maybe even a breaststroker. He had green eyes flecked with gold and thick black hair, an attractive combination with his smooth olive skin and pronounced nose, making the whole package rather striking.

"I hear you're my competition," he greeted, hand out to Jacob. His lightly accented English was better than good, almost like he'd lived in the States for a while. "Julio Espinosa. Breaststroke, Team Spain."

The name rang a bell, as did his appearance, from the last Olympics, but Julio couldn't have been much older than Jacob then, and Jacob had been so focused on—

He shook his head, focusing on the handsome man in front of him. "Jacob Burrows," he said, taking Julio's offered hand. "But you seem to know that already. And this"—he angled toward Leah—"is Leah Franklin, our women's breaststroke champ." Julio and Leah shook hands, Julio giving her an admiring smile.

"Our breaststroker, Sofia, is terrified of you." He waved at the statuesque blonde with Kevin.

"Good," Leah said. "I'm gonna go introduce myself." She gave Jacob a parting wink and faded into the crowd.

Julio inched closer, leaning a hip against the nearby chair. He folded his arms over his chest, muscles everywhere testing the seams of his shirt. One short sleeve rode up, a hint of ink peeking out from under its hem. "Gotta say, my competition is much more handsome in person."

He was smooth for sure, and attractive as hell, and if Jacob wasn't mistaken, flirting with him. Julio was putting himself out there without knowing if Jacob was gay or bi. Assertive, brave. Jacob liked that.

He didn't want to lead Leah on, hoping to keep her as a friend after the Olympics, but a two-week fling with this handsome fellow could be just what the doctor ordered to forget a certain other. Everyone was telling him to enjoy the experience. This was part of that, wasn't it?

Jacob smiled and leaned closer, desperately trying for cool. "Gotta say, I didn't expect my competition to be so handsome either."

BAS STOOD INSIDE the lounge doorway, overcome with a tsunami of *too old for this shit*. A giant room packed full of overhyped athletes, speakers pumping out dubstep that rattled his bones, and condoms being pocketed left and right. He was generally easygoing, never taking himself too seriously, but he was here to work, to backup Alex, and to make sure they won relay gold. Not babysit a rave. After a day of travel, pageantry, and avoiding Jacob, he just wanted to crash. Close his eyes, forget the day, and rewind to the night before in his mind, the only place where he'd let those memories live. He did not want to spend his evening here, reminded instead of a prior opening night gone wrong. As it was, he'd already glared off a pair of French swimmers and an Aussie pole vaulter he'd slept with four years ago.

"Ah, the hormones," Alex said, sidling up beside him.

On Alex's other side, Dane wrapped an arm around his boyfriend's waist. "I can talk to you about hormones," he teased.

"Nope, we're the adults here," Bas said.

Dane stuck out his bottom lip. "Well, that sucks. It's my first Olympics too. I don't get to have fun?" Big Red could act, Bas would give him that.

"Stop pouting," Alex said, failing miserably to sound stern. "Your boyfriend is captain. You signed on for this." Laughter bubbled beneath the surface of his words, belying the scolding.

Grinning, Dane leaned in and stole a kiss. "Okay, boyfriend."

Yeah, they liked that word, and Bas liked it for them, chuckling as he scanned the crowd for their teammates. No one in particular, he told himself, while searching for a shaved blond head. He spotted Kevin's glossy black pompadour first, standing in a circle chatting with Sean, Natalie, Leah, and a blonde he also vaguely remembered. Jacob, however, wasn't with them. Had they left him in the room? He'd thought he'd made it clear that he wanted Kevin and Sean to include Jacob. Had they offered, and Jacob declined, opting out of the opening-night party? Bas didn't want that either. As much as this scene rankled him, Jacob should still get the full experience.

Or maybe . . . Bas checked his watch. It was past the time for Jacob's nightly call with Davis. Was his dad all right? Had he had another flashback? By putting Jacob in a room with Sean and Kevin, Bas wouldn't know, wouldn't be there to help, if Jacob had another panic attack about his dad. *Fuck*, he needed to find out what was going on.

He turned to go, then froze as a familiar laugh pinged his ears, and on its heels, the owner of that same laugh, in a flirtatious tone Bas knew all too well, teasing, "I thought everything was bigger in Texas?"

Oh. Fuck. No.

Bas came unstuck, real fast. Like almost-took-down-Alex-and-Dane fast as he reversed course and plowed into the crowd.

"Bas!" Alex shouted over Dane's confused, "What the heck?"

Background noise, all of it. Pushing through the melee, Bas was locked on the two voices belonging to the last two people he'd ever wanted to meet each other. The sea of bodies parted.

Too late.

Julio was perched on the arm of Jacob's lounge chair, leaning in, hand braced on the seat back behind Jacob's head.

Spanish flirt turned way the fuck up.

And Jacob was falling for it, hook, line, and sinker. Who

wouldn't when Julio's charm was directed at you full blast? Cheeks pink, legs crossed toward the handsome Spaniard, Jacob's green eyes were bright and the big smile Bas had stolen was back where it belonged, stretching across his face.

"*¡Mierda!*" Alex cursed behind him.

Loud enough to register with Julio, who paused his seduction to glance up. He didn't lean back, though, just angled his face away from Jacob, gaze snagging on Alex, then Bas. Heated green-gold eyes clashed with his, too knowing for Bas's liking. Not how Bas wanted to first run into Julio again, angry when he had no right to be. But he was clearly hitting on Jacob, Bas's—

What? His what?

Teammate, mentee, and friend was the most he could say. The most *he'd* allowed. And Bas wasn't sure he'd even been a good any of those.

"Sebastian," Julio said, his accent drawing the name out to four syllables. Bas had loved that, until it had become his conscience's twenty-four-seven haunting.

"What the fuck do you think you're doing?"

"Bas!" Jacob exclaimed, eyes bulging out of his head.

Undeterred, Julio slid his arm farther behind Jacob, bringing them closer. "Just getting to know my competition better."

Bas wanted to shove him off the damn chair. "Oh, is that what you're doing?"

Entering the fray, Alex blocked Bas's step forward and extended a hand to Julio. "Espo, good to see you."

"Cantu, it's been too long."

Hand in his, Alex smoothly pulled Julio off the chair and into a bro hug. Bas's anger ratcheted down a gear.

"Thanks for accepting the friend request," Julio said, eyes cutting to Bas. He'd sent Bas one too, and also a direct message, both of which Bas had left ignored in his notifications.

Jacob stood, moving closer to Bas, and Bas's anger downshifted again, the tightness in his chest easing. "You all know each other?" Jacob asked.

Alex pushed Dane forward. "Julio, this my boyfriend, Dane Ellis."

"You two caused quite the stir," Julio said, shaking Dane's hand. "Glad not to be the center of attention this time. Between you two and the handsome rook here . . ." He leered again at Jacob.

Bas bit back a growl. "That's enough, J."

Julio smiled, not the least bit miffed. "Fine, then, go away," he said with a dismissive wave of his hand. "I'll get back to acquainting myself with Jacob."

Bas's growl escaped, rumbling into the tension-thick air between them. "No, you won't."

Julio's dark brows raced north and his smirk deepened. "Oh, it's like that, is it?"

Bas had shown his hand, exposing to the last person he should what Jacob might mean to him, whether Bas wanted that to be the case or not.

"You know Bas and Alex?" Jacob rephrased his earlier question. He motioned between them, his short sleeve creeping up, ink peeking out.

Julio's glowing eyes widened, no doubt putting puzzle pieces together. "We used to swim together at USC," he answered Jacob. "We were together at the last Olympics, until Bas—"

"Enough," Bas snapped. Fuck, he needed to get this situation under control before it spiraled into another incident like the one four years ago. "We're leaving," he said to Jacob, grabbing him by the upper arm.

Jacob wrenched free, expertly slipping his hold. "You leave. I'm staying." His emphasis on the last word landed like a punch to Bas's gut.

"Espo," Alex said. "How about we introduce you to some of the other new team members?" Another smooth move. At least someone still had their head about them, because Bas's was about to fucking explode.

Julio must have decided to save his own. "I'd like that," he conceded, but then inched his neck out again, tempting danger by asking Jacob, "You got my number?"

Jacob patted the pocket where he always kept his phone. "Got it."

"Use it." Julio cut another glance at Bas before he moved away with Alex.

As soon as the crowd swallowed them, Jacob rounded on Bas. "What the hell is wrong with you? You were beyond rude."

Bas lowered his voice, trying not to attract any more attention than they already had. "He's going to try and get into your head."

"Like he's already gotten into yours."

"This isn't about me, it's about you," he said, jabbing Jacob's chest with a finger. "He's your biggest competition. He's the best breaststroke swimmer in the world, and he's trying to fuck with you."

"Why do you think that?" Jacob crossed his arms, flexing. "Maybe he was just interested in me."

"Oh, he's interested all right."

"Why do you care?" Jacob bit back, the words a snarl unlike anything Bas had ever heard from him. "You won't even stay in the same room with me."

"I did that to better integrate you with the team."

"And back in Vienna?"

Another direct hit. Bas moved to step closer, to try to explain, and Jacob raised a hand between them.

"Give me one good reason to stay away from Julio."

"He's going to try and fuck with you."

"You already said that. Maybe it'd be good for me to get a read on him too. And if he wants to fuck me the other way . . ." He shrugged, playing nonchalant, even though his eyes burned with hurt and anger. "Our one night is over and done. You made that clear. You don't want another one."

Oh he wanted, more than Jacob knew and more than just one, but he was trying to keep from making the same mistake twice. For both their sakes. "You want a reason?" Bas yanked down the collar of his shirt, flashing the *JE* tattoo. "This is why he's going to fuck with you."

"J-E," Jacob mumbled, then twice more before his eyes grew huge, realization dawning. "Julio Espinosa."

"That's right. He's going to fuck with you because he's

my ex."

"Why's he going to fuck with me and not you, then?"

"Because I hurt him." Bas's gaze drifted from Jacob's confused eyes to the unwrapped tattoo on his shoulder. The damn giveaway. "And because he knows me too well."

CHAPTER
ELEVEN

JACOB STRUGGLED TO find his equilibrium after Bas's opening-night bombshell. Maybe if he hadn't been on the roller coaster from hell already, he'd have put it together before Bas had to lay it out for him. The rumors about Bas's breakup with his boyfriend at the last Olympics. The solitary, unadorned *JE* over his heart. Tall, dark, and charming Julio Espinosa.

Julio was the sort of man Bas belonged with, a perfect contrast to Bas's blond, blue eyed, laid-back vibe. Not gangly, gawky, uncool, inexperienced Jacob. God, he'd broken down three nights ago, told Bas he was a virgin, and begged Bas to fuck him. Whatever had precipitated Bas and Julio's breakup four years ago, Jacob would bet it wasn't because Julio was pathetic.

That was about all Jacob could deduce though, since Bas had bolted after flashing his tattoo and avoided anything but swim talk the past two days. Jacob was a zombie with all the tossing and turning, second-guessing, and what-the-fucks that were running like a twenty-four-hour Whataburger drive-thru in his head. Heartburn guaranteed. He was surprised neither Kevin nor Sean had kicked him out yet, between the insomnia and the moping. He was definitely violating the number-one rule, bringing the room's vibe down.

Yesterday's third-place finish in his hundred-meter breaststroke heat didn't help matters. At least he'd done well enough to make today's final. Alex had given him a pep talk afterward, and they'd analyzed tape yesterday afternoon to see where he could improve. Jacob didn't want to take Alex away from Dane or from prepping for his own races, but the natural teacher in Alex had seemed to need an outlet, and it had calmed Jacob, if only temporarily. He felt somewhat more confident, if still sleep-deprived, going into tonight's race.

Until he stepped out of the locker room. The thunderous crowd noise echoed all the way down the athlete's tunnel to the locker room, the cement and glass construction of the Madrid Aquatic Center amplifying everything.

The gigantic indoor natatorium had the same bright Mediterranean aesthetic as Olympic Village. While it was technically indoors, the white cement and glass walls, polished sandstone deck, and blue-bottomed pool made it feel like a tropical sandy beach.

During his morning heat yesterday, it had been like the coast in spring and fall, only lightly populated. By the roaring chants tonight, it was Fourth of July out there. Jacob supposed tonight's race lineup—the semifinals of the two-hundred-meter freestyle and one-hundred-meter backstroke, then the final medal races of the one-hundred-meter

breaststroke and four-by-one-hundred free relay—
guaranteed every seat in the house would be filled. It had
sucked to have a poor showing in front of the lighter crowd
yesterday; it'd suck a whole lot worse to bomb in front of the
full house tonight, not to mention everyone who'd watch
back home in the States.

"No pressure or anything."

Whipping around, Jacob spotted Julio leaning against
the wall behind him. He'd managed to avoid Julio yesterday,
swimming in separate heats, and in the locker room today by
showing up at the last possible second. Julio, though, must
have been lingering in the sun-cast shadows of the athletes'
tunnel, the only dark spot in the place. He drew alongside
Jacob, as they made their way toward the pool. "It's a lot to
take in for a first timer, especially on a squad favored to win.
You don't want to let the guys down."

As if Jacob needed the reminder.

"Don't let the bright lights distract you," Julio added.

"Thought that's what you were trying to do."

A slow smile spread across his handsome face. "Ah, so
Bas told you I'm the bad guy."

"He said you'd try to fuck with me."

Julio's smile tilted into a leer. "Well, yeah, I had thought
about that."

So had Jacob—the Spaniard's radiating charm and good
looks reeling him in the other night—but no way was he
touching Julio with a ten-foot pole, now knowing his history
with Bas. Things were awkward enough already.

"I heard you two broke up at the last Olympics," Jacob

said. "Bas also said he hurt you."

Julio faltered a step, genuine surprise flitting across his face. "Did he now? You get the full story or you need me to fill you in?"

"Right now, I just need to swim."

The athletes' tunnel dumped them out in front of the first row of bleachers, behind an eight-foot wall of glass in an area where they held the swimmers for the next event. Out of the shadowy tunnel, Jacob squinted against the brightness. At one end of the pool, there was an entire wall of green-tinted glass, the multilevel concourse visible behind it. Raised arena seats ran up the other three sides of the event area, another ten feet of windows above those, and an industrial metal roof capped off the place. Sunlight streamed in during day events, and for the night races, the arena lights blazed bright.

The deck itself was clean and minimalist, blocks at either end and a single row of white stone benches, where coaches and captains crowded together with their swimmers. Beside one of those blocks, Alex was hauling Dane out of the pool after the latter's semifinal heat. Already roaring at Dane's record setting pace, the crowd roared louder when Dane snaked an arm around Alex's waist and kissed him.

Jacob had heard mention of them waiting for a public kiss until after winning the medley relay gold, but that had clearly been tossed out the window, the both of them too happy to hold it in.

Beside Jacob, Julio leaned closer to be heard over the noise. "I still can't believe those two got together."

Jacob would have dismissed the attempt at conversation if not for the pure, unguarded smile and genuine admiration in the other man's voice. He was happy for Alex and Dane, and why wouldn't he be? Julio had swum with Alex at USC. They used to be friends and teammates, before the last Olympics.

"Did you know they were together, before?" Jacob asked.

"I didn't know it was Dane Ellis, but I knew there was someone in Alex's past that had hurt him."

Julio's smile wavered, and Jacob sensed he wasn't only talking about Alex. Jacob added that reaction to what Bas had said the other night, trying to make the equation work. "Whatever Bas did, I think he regrets it."

Julio laughed, a bitter note underlying the attractive sound. "Doesn't do me much good now, does it? I needed him then."

Like Jacob needed Bas now. His stomach soured at the balanced equation.

"Ah, left you in his wake already, has he? Well, that changes things . . ."

Jacob's insides clenched at the shift in Julio's gaze, those dark eyes calculating. They knotted further when Julio turned, shucking his jacket, and Jacob got a good look at his bared back and shoulders.

That was why he remembered Julio Espinosa from the last Olympics. Because he had a tattoo on his back left delt, intricate flowing line work that Jacob would recognize anywhere now. Whereas his was a Texas Longhorn, Julio's tattoo was an abstract rose, tipped in gold and red, and the

Spanish rose's stem had the unmistakable bend of California to it, with a heart-shaped leaf where LA would be. It shouldn't work, but somehow it did, because Bas was that damn talented of an artist.

But that wasn't the tattoo that made Jacob reach out and brace a hand on the dividing glass. It was the simple *SS* on the outside of Julio's other shoulder, the ends of which he'd just barely glimpsed beneath Julio's sleeve the other night. An exact match in font and style to the *JE* over Bas's heart.

Sebastian Stewart.

Julio Espinosa.

Jacob was still staring when Alex and Dane came through the holding area's swinging glass door. "Was that Julio?" Dane asked.

"Yeah," Jacob said, then to Alex, "I need you tell me what happened between him and Bas at the last Olympics."

A shadow fell over Alex's face, despite the abundance of light in the giant building. "Jacob, you have to be in the water in ten minutes."

"Alex, tell me, please."

"Pup, this isn't the time or place. You need to swim."

He pointed at Julio's back. "Look at that tattoo."

Alex angled his face the opposite direction. "I don't need to. I was there when Bas inked it."

"*And* he's got Bas's initials on his shoulder." Jacob dropped his hand from the wall. "I've got no chance in this race if my mind is wandering three lanes over, wondering what the hell happened between those two. I thought I could block it out, but after seeing Julio's ink, I can't."

"You don't—" Dane started.

Jacob cut him off. "Alex, please."

Deflating, Alex nodded and led them back into the shadows of the tunnel, out of the way of the other passing swimmers. "Go," he said to Dane. "You've got another race tonight." Dane hesitated, eyeing Jacob warily, until Alex physically pushed him toward the locker room.

Once Dane was inside, Alex turned back around. "You gotta understand, Pup, Bas blames himself for what happened, and a lot of the blame rests there, justifiably, but there was a lot more going on too. Mo's wife was having a baby, Kevin and Sean were first timers, and I was too focused on the meet to realize how much trouble we were all in. We're a team, and the team did not have each other's backs. That's why we harp on it now."

Jacob appreciated the sentiment, but at this point, he was ready to rip his too-fucking-short hair out. "Alex, please, just tell me what happened."

Alex hung his head, finally caving. "Espo was an exchange student at SC, swam with me and Bas. They were infatuated with each other from first glance." Jacob's stomach did another of those awful flips, and then it kept flipping, like in a car accident, as Alex went on with the story. "They dated for two years, though not without issues. Espo always wanted more, and Bas held him off. Espo was also a terrible flirt, and he never seemed comfortable with Bas being bi, so maybe Bas didn't trust him either. In any event, Espo went home to Spain to train for the Olympics, and when he and Bas met back up after a couple months apart, he forced the issue, showing up with that tattoo." Alex tapped his outer arm, where Julio's SS tattoo was inked. "Made a big show of revealing it to Bas in front of everyone at the opening-night party. Bas reacted poorly, to say the least. He shot Espo down and walked out of the lounge with a pair of French swimmers, one on each arm. I don't think he slept in the same room once the entire two weeks we were there."

Bile stung the back of Jacob's throat. "And Julio saw all that?"

Alex nodded. "Bas wasn't exactly discrete. He was making a point, albeit poorly. Julio couldn't ignore it, and it threw him off. He was the favorite, and he failed to medal in any of his races, and even though Bas wouldn't admit it, that tore him up even more. He did care for Espo, but rather than apologize, he partied more. He was so sleep-deprived and unfocused that it threw our team off as well. He showed up to the medley relay final five minutes before introductions. We were lucky to win silver."

Jacob sank back against the tunnel wall, wishing he hadn't asked. He supposed he should be thankful Bas hadn't made any sort of scene like that between them, or rubbed other lovers in his face, but he couldn't help wondering if Bas was willing to give Julio a second chance, if he'd been that infatuated. And that regretful. Jacob himself had told Julio he thought Bas regretted it. He also couldn't help wondering if he was a pawn, being played between the two of them. And why the hell would either bother with inexperienced him? Hell, they were so far out of his league, it was ridiculous.

That overwhelming sense of being out of his league sharpened as Jacob stood on the Lane 1 starting block, glancing down the row at the other seven swimmers who had all been here before. Julio—the world's best, Bas had called him—was coiled like a snake atop the Lane 4 block. What made Jacob think he ever belonged here, at the Olympics, much less on the US medley relay team? He was the one dragging the team down this time around.

Limbs tight, stomach in his throat, head not at all in the race, only instinct propelled him off the block when the starting horn blew. His launch was a split-second late, though, and not as powerful as it should have been. Then he came out of the water too soon, just like he'd been doing in the botched practices in Vienna. He played catch-up the entire race, not thinking about his own swim but the speed and experience of every other swimmer in the pool. And certain other swimmers out of it.

There was nothing to look forward to ahead, nothing to bring him home. Each inhale, each push of his arms and legs, became a battle. He couldn't catch his breath, and he couldn't catch the world's best who'd beaten him off the blocks. The packed house was watching *the kid* do what he did best.

Choke.

CHAPTER
TWELVE

"JACOB, DO YOU think you can come back from that disastrous medal race yesterday?"

"What went wrong?"

"Can the team still win relay gold?"

Five minutes into their Olympic Media Day panel and Bas was ready to leap across the table and do bodily harm to more than one reporter. If he hadn't been in this fucking suit, he probably would have already.

Each thinly veiled or not-veiled-at-all accusation flung at Jacob pierced Bas's chest like an arrow. The press had gone from fawning all over the new talent after opening ceremonies, to crucifying Jacob today. Bas reconsidered the secret-weapon strategy; it had ended up hurting Jacob more than it'd protected him. The pup took each hit with a jolt, growing paler by the question, and the arrows in Bas's chest continued to twist, ripping apart his insides.

This was his fault, not Jacob's. He was the reason Jacob had been off yesterday. Not that Jacob had done anything to be ashamed of. He'd had a bad start and swam from behind to take bronze. At nineteen, he'd stood on an Olympic podium. How many of these reporters could say that?

Bas reached for the mic to say as much, but Alex beat him to it.

"Respectfully"—Bas didn't think Alex needed to give the press that much, but that was why Alex was the captain—"my teammate, at his *first* Olympics, medaled in his *first* race. At nineteen, I'd say that's pretty damn impressive. I have complete confidence in Jacob, in his next race and in the medley relay. Now, let's move on."

"Surely, you've got other questions for us," Dane drawled on the other side of Alex, inviting the obvious.

Taking the bait, the reporters shifted focus to Alex and Dane. Jacob, however, leaned forward and reached for a mic.

Bas clasped his knee under the table. "You don't have to, Pup."

"Yeah, I kinda do." His gaze was wary but determined. "Y'all can't take responsibility for me. I'm the one dragging the team down, and I need to fix it. I can only count on me."

He pushed Bas's hand off his knee, and an arrow twisted all the way to Bas's heart. Jacob *knew*, the entire story. Someone—Julio, Sean or Kevin, or Alex—had told him. Not that it was a secret. Bas had made a pretty public mess of things four years ago. He should have been the one to tell Jacob, but he'd avoided him, ashamed of himself, for past and present acts, for taking advantage. More than that, if he'd told Jacob and Jacob had forgiven him, asked him to stay despite being a complete jackass, Bas wasn't certain he could have resisted. And if he didn't resist, and he made a mess of things again, he'd be the one putting Jacob and the medley relay gold at risk, again.

There was no worry of Jacob asking him to stay now. He knew the truth, saw the real Bas, and the disappointment was reflected in his big green eyes. Eyes that had once looked at Bas with admiration and desire. Not any longer.

"Actually, I'd like to say something."

Jacob's amplified voice snapped Bas back to the present.

The pup squared his shoulders and took a giant breath, steeling himself. "Yesterday wasn't my best performance. These guys—" he gestured left and right "—warned me about the Olympic experience being overwhelming."

"Gotta second him there," Dane interjected, and the crowd tittered.

The tension in Jacob's frame eased a little, and Bas would have hugged Dane if he weren't two chairs away.

"It got the better of me yesterday," Jacob said. "For my team, and for myself, I plan to—*hope to* do better in my next race and in the medley relay. I know how important the medley relay gold is to these guys and the team. I don't want to let them down."

Questions broke out, follow-ups on practice times and other races, and Alex and Coach, on the other side of Dane, took over fielding them. Bas wanted to reach for Jacob. A hand on his shoulder—something, *anything*—to indicate how proud he was of him, that he was confident Jacob would live up to his words, but the way Jacob held himself slightly apart, like he anticipated it, kept Bas from acting on the instinct. One he needed to quash anyway.

Plastering on a smile, Bas checked back into the press

conference, answering the few questions directed at him and slipping in encouraging words where warranted. Past the questions about Jacob's first race, the rest of the panel went fine, nothing like the chaotic Media Day in San Antonio. After it was done, Coach called Jacob over before Bas could get a word in with him. Bas turned to Alex instead, their backs to the mic. "How much does he know?"

"He asked yesterday, before the race, after he got a look at Espo's ink."

"Fuck!" He ran a hand over his head, bumping into his top knot. "Julio saw his tat at the party. He'd have recognized the work. Known that I'd inked the pup already."

"Jacob's not the only US swimmer with your artwork on his body."

"I inked him *before* the meet, Alejandro."

Dane leaned his head in. "And Bas doesn't look at any other swimmers the way he looks at Jacob."

Bas speared him with a deadly glare.

Dane lifted his hands. "Hey, just telling the truth."

"He's not lying," Alex piled on. "Julio would have also seen you two at opening ceremonies. Your . . . concern . . . was obvious."

Fucking hell. "How much did you tell him?"

Before Alex could answer, there was a commotion in front of the dais. By Dane's sudden rigidity, Bas could guess at the cause of the ruckus.

A too-saccharine voice, a more affected version of Dane's Southern drawl, confirmed it. "Dane, honey, we'd like a word with you." Kimberly Ellis, in four-figure Chanel Bas recognized from his own mother's recently expanded closet, looked her camera-ready, home-shopping-queen self. Standing next to her, Reverend Patrick Ellis, "the country's minister" many called him, was in his standard three-piece getup, a fire-and-brimstone scowl on his face.

Dane wove his fingers together with Alex's. "I have nothing to say to you."

The Reverend's upper lip curled, but Mrs. Ellis stayed the course. "We have some things to work out. You're still our son."

"Not by your own words," Bas said. He'd been in the room when the Ellises had disowned their only child. "Witnesses are a bitch."

Jacob reappeared at their sides, clamping a hand over the closest table mic. "We're drawing a crowd. How about we take this someplace private?"

"We don't need to hear from you," Patrick clipped.

"These are my teammates, so I'm afraid you do, sir."

Jacob's *sir* and heavier-than-usual Texas accent were a stroke of genius. Polite, respectful, and bridging the gap with the Ellises, even if Bas didn't think they deserved the consideration. But Alex and Dane also didn't deserve to have their dirty laundry aired in public, more than it already had been.

"Burrows is right," Coach said, joining them. "There's a conference room down the hall we can use." He held out an arm toward stage left and the exit door.

Descending the steps, Jacob had them wait at the bottom while Dane's parents passed. Another show of respect.

Amidst this chaos, the return of Jacob's hyperobservance comforted Bas. This was the pup's game face. Bas needed to get his own head back in the game, the one happening right now, where everything was on the line for Alex and Dane. As they walked behind the Ellises, he pulled out his phone and texted his mother.

Last in, Bas pushed the door to, leaving it slightly cracked. Turning, he caught Jacob's gaze, those green eyes hard and determined, a protective mode he must have perfected on his father's behalf. How strong had Jacob had to be? For how long? And how had he juggled that with everything else? Well, he didn't have to juggle alone in this case. Bas schooled his features similarly, nodded, and they joined the group around the conference table, fighting together for their friends and teammates.

"I thought it was pretty clear last time we spoke that we were through," Dane said.

"Emotions were running high," Mrs. Ellis said.

"And they aren't now?"

The door swung open and Sasha Stewart strode in. Near six feet tall and working the curves the deity gave her, his mother was a riot of color in her rainbow linen suit, with red, white, and blue braids woven into her blond hair. Mrs. Ellis looked positively offended. Bas bit back a proud smile.

"You received the legal paperwork," she said, blue eyes begging for a fight. "That should address everything." Bas's mom had drafted all the documents necessary to move Dane's assets, including his sponsorships, into a new trust that his parents couldn't touch. As stressful as this was for

Dane, it was a walk in the park for Sasha, having emancipated more than a few young stars from their controlling managers and parents.

"I'm guessing that's why they're really here," Alex said.

"Do I need to read the documents to you, line by line?" Sasha asked. "Or we can call your attorney. Get him on the line too."

"That was a drastic measure, son," Mrs. Ellis said, addressing Dane instead.

"To safeguard my—" he lifted his and Alex's clasped hands "—*our* future."

Reverend Ellis's scowl deepened.

"Dane's trust isn't the real problem, is it?" Jacob said. Bas didn't miss the undercurrent of judgment belying the good-ole-boy accent. Jacob was lulling them into a false sense of security and setting a trap. "You're standing there, across the table, as far away from Alex and Bas as possible, and you haven't even tried to hug Dane, your son who you're supposedly here to reconnect with. Do you think they'll bite? That their sexuality, your son's sexuality, somehow endangers you? Or are you just that repulsed by us, for no good reason?"

Their eyes widened, catching on that the nice young Southern boy was also queer. "It's like you're all brainwashed," Mrs. Ellis murmured, while Patrick looked aghast at Coach. "What kind of team are you running here?"

"A winning one," Hartl replied.

"Full of f—"

"Don't go there," Bas growled, as he strained not to

launch across a table a second time today. Flexing all his muscles, he cursed and thanked the suit that made his fly swimmer's mass—the biggest in the room already—seem twice as large.

Patrick quelled, a bit.

"You wasted your time and money coming here," Dane said. "You still don't get it. They"—he held his arms out wide—"didn't change me. You're the ones who tried to do that. They accepted me. These are my brothers, my team, my family now." He clasped Alex's hand again, and Bas slung an arm over Dane's shoulders from the other side.

Jacob's fingers nudged and tangled with his, and if not for that too-tight suit, Bas was sure his heart would've beaten right out of his chest. It was a show of solidarity for Dane— and Bas didn't let his gaze stray, maintaining the same—but that touch meant everything. More than it should.

"Sign the papers," Sasha said. "So Dane and Alex can move on with their lives."

"We won't let this happen," Patrick said. "There are places—"

"Over my dead body." The violence in Alex's voice could have slain armies.

Bas saw the return fire on the tip of Reverend Ellis's tongue. He should let him make it, but he didn't want Alex or Dane to suffer that. Lowering his arm, he dug his hand into his pocket and pulled out his phone. He tossed it on the table, screen up, recorder showing. "Go ahead, say it. I'm sure threats of that sort will be more than enough to get a restraining order on top of the divestiture. Your golden goose is gone. Hope you saved some of that TV money for retirement."

Bas's mother smiled over at him. "Nice work, son."

Jacob fired the final shot, polite yet no less deadly. "I think we're done here. Please go and leave my friends alone. We've got all we need here." His fingers tightened around Bas's, and Bas squeezed back, thumb sweeping his knuckles.

In the face of their united front, the Ellises tucked their tails and retreated, mumbling huffed *goodbyes* and meaningless *take care*s on their way out.

"You good?" Coach asked, eyeing Dane. "I need to go make sure they don't cause a scene out there."

"We got it here," Bas said, as Dane added, "Appreciate it, Coach. And thanks, Ms. Stewart."

"Of course." She patted Bas's shoulder, then headed for the door behind Hartl. "I'm going to see if I can get them to sign those papers."

Once the door swung closed, Dane rotated and rested back against the table, hands covering his face. Jacob untangled from Bas and went to Dane, and Bas turned his attention to a still-trembling Alex.

He'd known the mention of conversion camps would set Alex off. At SC, they'd counseled kids who'd survived those inhumane programs. And *survived* was the right word. Now, *that* was brainwashing, and it was a long, hard road back from it. Alex reacted predictably, justifiably, when the man he loved was threatened with torture. If someone had threatened Jacob with that . . . Bas banished the thought, and the next instant, the implication he'd just drawn.

He focused on Alex instead, rubbing a hand over his friend's shoulders. "*Cálmate, cálmate,*" he murmured.

Dane dropped his hands. "I'm sorry they got in the middle again."

"At least they waited until after the presser," Bas said. "Without a scene this time, relatively."

"Thank you," Dane said, glancing up at Jacob. "For diverting that."

Jacob shrugged. "Seemed best for everyone."

Dane nodded. "You did good, Pup. Thanks."

"So did you, Ellis," Bas said. "How's that backbone feel?"

"Good," he said with a small smile. Pushing off the table, he crossed to Alex and pulled him into his arms. Only then did Alex finally start to relax, shoulders lowering from his ears and jaw unclenching. "Easier knowing all of you have it," Dane said over his boyfriend's head. "Thank you."

Bas's eyes locked with Jacob's. "It's what family does."

ONLY ATHLETES, TRAINERS, and coaches were permitted in Olympic Village, yet somehow Bas's mother had finagled her way inside and claimed one of the picnic tables by the pond. She sat, one leg crossed over the other, sipping from a coffee cup and looking supremely satisfied with herself.

Shucking his jacket and rolling up his sleeves, Bas straddled the bench across the table from her. "How did you get in here?"

She glanced at him over the top of her designer shades. "I have my ways."

"You sweet-talked Coach, didn't you?"

She shrugged, feigning innocence, and pushed the coffee cup across the table to him. "I sweet-talk people for a living."

"Oh," Bas said. "Is that what you call what you just did to the Ellises?"

"No, that's what I call justice."

Bas tilted the cup toward her. "I'll drink to that." He took a sip—Turkish black, his and her favorite. "So they signed the papers?"

She pushed her shades up onto her head and ruffled her dyed bangs. "Their lawyer is 'reviewing them.'" The last was said with air quotes and a roll of her blue eyes, the same as Bas's. "They'll sign them. And Dane knows not to sign any new contracts until they do. I also have connections to several of Kimberly Ellis's sponsors, so if she holds those papers hostage much longer, I'll return the favor. She'll have nothing to sell on that precious show of hers except those creepy-as-fuck porcelain figurines."

Bas reached across the table, grasping his wonderful mother's hand. "I'm glad you're here, Mom."

She curled her fingers around his, then withdrew her hand to gesture at their surroundings. "I missed all this last time. Wasn't about to miss it again."

Four years ago, she'd been in the middle of one of her firm's biggest cases. She'd needed to stay, and Bas hadn't thought twice about backing her decision. A divorcee who'd lost her house and half her pension to an adulterous husband, Sasha Stewart had battled depression while raising him on a legal secretary's shoestring budget, putting all her spare change to swim and art lessons. Once he'd been old enough to get jobs sweeping floors at the local tattoo parlor and lifeguarding at the pool where he trained, she'd gone to night school, earned a law degree, then landed a job at one of LA's best firms. She'd been on the cusp of winning a career-making case, one for a mom-in-need, much like she had been. She'd needed that case more than he'd needed her at his meet. In retrospect, Bas was glad she hadn't been there to witness him acting like an idiot.

He was glad to have her at this one, though, her schedule more flexible now, thanks to an army of associates. "Perks of being a partner?" he said.

She winked, stealing back the coffee cup. "One of the few." When she lowered it, Bas didn't like the devious look in her eyes one bit. "So . . ." She tapped the plastic coffee lid with her long acrylic nails, painted with an eagle and the Olympic rings. "You want to tell me about that other sweet Southern boy you couldn't keep your eyes off of?"

"It's not like that," he said automatically. He hoped that would be the end of it.

It wasn't. "He couldn't keep his eyes off you either. He's queer, yeah?"

He stripped out of his suit coat and unknotted his tie. "Yeah, bi, like me."

"Thought I caught that. So why's it 'not like that,' then?"

When he didn't answer, she reached out and grabbed the end of his tie, flicking it up into his face with a motherly,

"Sebastian."

Sometimes it sucked to have a legal shark as his mother. And as his other best friend. He could never lie to her. Maybe if she had been here last time, some things, like the mess he'd made with Julio, would have gone differently. Maybe he should talk to her about Jacob, now that she was.

He propped an elbow on the table, chin in his hand. "He's too good for me."

She flitted her hand with a *pssh* added for effect. "You're always too hard on yourself." One of the things he loved best about his mom was that she'd never pressured him to be anything. She accepted him for who he was. Full stop. But she also had a motherly blind spot.

"No, Mom, really. Jacob's smart, selfless, talented, beautiful, and hyperobservant."

"That'll work for you in bed."

He covered his face with his hand, groaning.

She rapped his knuckles with her nails. "Hey, if you can't talk to your mother about these things . . ."

He peeked through his fingers. "I don't think most people talk to their mother about these things."

She waved at her hair and suit, then over at his dreads and tattoos. "We're not most people. And if Jacob's as good as you say, snatch him up. You already let Alex get away."

Not that he'd ever wanted Alex that way, no matter how much she'd wanted his best friend as a son-in-law. But it was the sentence before that got to the heart of the matter.

"That's just it, Mom. Jacob deserves commitment. He's been left behind before, and I can't do that to him. I don't want to hurt anyone the way Dad hurt you."

The thought of Jacob crying on the shower floor like his mother, water long gone cold, tore at his insides. The thought that maybe it had already been that bad for Jacob, at his hand or someone else's, made him want to hurl.

"I swore off marriage and commitment the day Dad left. I was a fool to give it a try with Julio, and I don't want to do that to someone else."

"What makes you think you would?"

He held up a hand, ticking off the offenders. "Dad, Granddad, Great-granddad, me, if we wanna talk about the way I broke things off with Julio."

"That was you being a stupid punk kid. You're allowed to make mistakes. That's how we learn."

"Is that why you never married again?"

She shook her head. "I never married again because no one was good enough for *you*. And for my own reasons. I was raised to believe I had to marry and depend on a man. That didn't go too good, obviously. So after the divorce, once I got past the worst of the depression, I vowed to stand on my own two feet before I'd ever consider marrying again. I got to the top of the mountain, on my own, and I like it here. I needed to do that, *for me*."

"And now?"

Her eyes got that devious glint about them again. "I like sweet-talking that Coach of yours."

He laughed out loud, the thought hilarious, yet not without merit.

But his mother, ever the lawyer, still had to deliver her

closing statement. "That's me, Bas, but you, my child, are not cut out for being single forever. You're an artist, you see beauty everywhere, and you need inspiration, especially love. You work a job where you're around people all the time." She sat the empty cup aside and covered his hands. "Don't you want to make your own art, your own life, with inspiration by your side every day? With someone you think is beautiful, inside and out?"

It was a convincing argument. Jacob was all those things, and Bas would like nothing more than to have that kind of beauty in his life every day, but in keeping it there, he feared he'd wreck the very thing he wanted most.

CHAPTER
THIRTEEN

SITTING UP IN bed, awake for the past couple of hours, Jacob stared out the open window, watching as the sun spread across the Spanish hills, spilled over the sandstone Olympic Complex, and crept toward Madrid's city center. Rays had just reached the border of the tightly packed buildings when church bells rang from all directions, a symphony playing the start of a new day.

Jacob glanced over his shoulder. Neither Sean nor Kevin stirred. Sean was used to the morning bells from his previous time in Europe, and Kevin had gotten used to them last week in Vienna. Jacob usually beat them both awake, unable to stop his mind from racing for more than a few hours a night. Used to be, he'd hit the water at a meet and zone out, focused on swimming, and he'd be so tired afterward he'd crash. But that had all changed with this meet.

All those warnings about the Olympics were true, except his drama had started weeks ago, before they'd even got here, and the pressure had mounted steadily. He had a heat later this morning, which after his statement at the press conference, he needed to win. And he had a teammate he didn't know whether to confront or dodge, especially after their handhold yesterday. They'd been standing together, against Dane's parents, but it'd felt like he and Bas had turned a corner. Like maybe things would improve. But he'd thought that after their night together in Vienna too. One night of better before it'd all gotten much worse. Jacob didn't know if he had it in him to hope for better again and crash back to reality a second time.

And then there was also Julio, who was swimming in his heat today.

Jacob sank back down, intending to hide under the covers a little while longer. He'd tugged the sheets as far as his chin when banging on the door joined the symphony of bells from outside.

"You up, Pup?" Dane called through the door.

Whipping back the sheet, Jacob scurried out of bed, tripping over his own shoes as he reached for his T-shirt. He righted himself and dug through his bag, searching for a pair of sweats.

The banging started again. "Yo, Pup!"

Sean lifted his head, eyes half-open. "What the fuck?"

"I got it, I got it," Jacob said, giving up the search for the sweats. He hurried to the door and cracked it open, finger to his lips. "Shh, you'll wake the dead."

Dane smiled, way too chipper for six in the morning. "Good, you're up."

"I am now."

"Lies, you were already awake." He waggled a finger at his face. "No eye crusties. You're with me this morning."

Jacob opened the door wider, leaning on the edge. "Do-ing what?"

"Cooking breakfast. I'm tired of the cafeteria shit."

"It's not been shit." The menu had been chosen, cali-brated, and prepared for an athlete's diet.

Dane gave him a baleful look. "It's been boring as fuck."

Jacob chuckled, resting his head against his hand. "Not everyone is an amateur chef."

The door across the hall opened, and Bas poked his head out. Dreads loose, face soft with sleep, Jacob couldn't help but stare. And want. And hope Bas was in there alone. Still half-asleep, Bas didn't seem to notice his ogling, scratching his chest and making the temptation worse. "Are you two going to have a whole conversation out here?"

"If we have to," Dane said.

Bas turned to Jacob, eyes half-lidded. "Pup, whatever it is, do what he says. Please." He shut the door, and Jacob wished he was on the other side of it with him. Not standing over the threshold of his triple, arguing with the red-headed rooster.

"He's swimming today," Dane said. "So is Alex. I want to do this for them."

And Jacob wanted to crawl back in bed for a couple more hours of shut-eye before his heat, but Dane looked so damn earnest. "You're swimming too," he said, not forget-ting Dane's freestyle relay final tonight. "So are they," he added with a tilt of his head back to the room where his roommates slept.

Dane sighed dramatically. "Fine, we can make enough

for them too."

"Where are we going to do this? You can't just bust into the Village cafeteria and mess up their routine."

"The kitchenette on the other end of the floor." That could work. It had all the cooking basics—fridge, stove, microwave, sink, a couple of tables. Athletes kept and cooked what they needed there for their personalized diets, in addition to the big cafeteria's more general offerings.

"What do you need me for? You're the chef."

"I need your pickpocket skills to filch some things from the main kitchen."

Jacob banged his head on his hand. He knew swiping Coach's training center card back in the States was going to come back to haunt him. He just didn't think it would be like this.

"Come on, Pup. It's for a good cause." He peeked through his lashes at a grinning Dane. "Live a little."

Turn the corner.

Jacob sighed, because the drama queen deserved it thrown back at him. "Let me find my sweats and brush my teeth."

Dane smiled big, not the publicity one, the real one he'd been flashing more often since coming out and reuniting with Alex. Jacob, improbably, was smiling too as he ducked back into his room. He finally found his sweats, on the floor next to his bag, and quickly washed up in the bathroom.

He nearly ran into Sean on his way out. "What'd Big Red want?"

"To cook breakfast."

"'Bout fucking time we got some real food up in here."

"Who said you were invited?"

Sean raked a hand through his dark hair, making it even more of an unruly mess than it already had been. "Haven't we been good to you, Pup?"

Jacob stepped past him, hand on his shoulder. "Yeah, you have. Which is why I already put you on the list." Sean held his fist out for a bump. "Lounge in an hour," Jacob said, bumping back. "And get him up too." He jutted a thumb at Kevin before slipping out the door.

Dane was across the hall, chatting with Bas, who stood leaning against his doorframe in just his boxer-briefs, dreads up, looking more awake. Looking gorgeous. "Hey," Bas said, and Jacob jerked his gaze up from where it'd wandered south. "How you doing today?"

"You should get some more sleep," Jacob replied. "Hour before we eat."

"By those bags under your eyes, I'd say you need more sleep too." He turned his blue gaze on Dane. "You really need him for this adventure?"

"I'm fine," Jacob said. "I'll take a nap later today, after I swim."

Disbelieving eyes swung back his way, but Dane swooped in with the save. "Let's go, Pup," he said. "While we can still sneak in and out of the cafeteria. Bas, grab Alex on your way."

"Will do. Try not to get caught."

Jacob felt Bas's gaze lingering on his back until the stairwell door shut behind him. His comment apparently also lingered with Dane. "He's right," the freestyler said, once they hit the promenade outside. "You look like shit."

"Gee, thanks."

"For real, Pup."

"I haven't been sleeping great." Jacob didn't hold back as much with Dane. He figured Dane appreciated the truth more than most, especially after spending so much of his life surrounded and controlled by lies. And in a way, they were the two on the outside looking in, on Bas and Alex, on the team, and on the Olympics.

"How are you doing, really?" Dane asked, as they walked through the morning quiet of Olympic Village.

"You pulled the short straw, huh?"

Dane's brow furrowed. "What do you mean?"

Jacob pointed at himself. "Dealing with the messed-up kid."

"Not at all. This is me thanking you for yesterday. And like I said at the presser, I'm a first timer too. Don't know about you, but all this—" he waved a hand at their surroundings "—sure as heck is getting to me."

Jacob halted midstep. "Seriously? Because you don't show it."

"My past as a windup doll for my parents does occasionally come in handy." He plastered on the fake smile and gave a beauty pageant wave his mother would be proud off.

Jacob doubled over laughing; it felt good. When he righted himself, Dane was smiling his real smile again. They were so clearly distinguishable, Jacob was shocked no one had been able to tell before. Had his true one really been

159

tucked away that long?

"Don't tell Alex," Dane said, as they set off again. "But that's also why I'm cooking this morning. I need to do and think about something else besides yesterday."

"I get that," Jacob said, nodding. "But the nerves, really? You've been in the spotlight forever."

Dane shrugged. "We lost a teammate, almost lost our captain, I came out, you left the country for the first time, Bas's ex showed up."

"Ugh, don't remind me."

"You couldn't have known," Dane said, as they reached their destination.

With only minutes to spare before the cooks arrived, there was minimal talking as Jacob worked fast, picking the lock as his father had taught him, first on cars, then other doors. Inside, Dane quickly gathered what they needed, Jacob holding open a bag for him as he dumped things in: peppers, onion, garlic, chorizo, cheese, a piecrust, a few more odds and ends, and a dozen eggs placed carefully on top.

They were back in the lounge kitchenette, Jacob cracking eggs, when he asked, "How did you know?"

"Know what?"

"That Alex was the one."

Dane's knife didn't falter in its quick, precise cuts through a bell pepper. "You're not thinking of Julio, are you?"

"God, no." Just the thought made Jacob beat the eggs harder.

Grinning, Dane moved on to the onion, his dicing skill

and speed downright scary. "I wanted to be near Alex. Always. Even when we were apart. Even when I thought I hated him."

Jacob understood that feeling, maybe not to the depth Dane did for Alex, separated from each other for ten years, but he missed Bas. Hell, he hadn't slept well since the night he'd slept like the dead in Bas's arms.

"Now I can't imagine being apart," Dane said, as he tossed the peppers and onion into an oiled skillet with a smashed clove of garlic.

"Do you regret it? Coming out?"

"I know it's going to be hard, but no. It's what both of us needed." He added the chorizo to the pan, mixing it with the peppers, onions, and garlic. "You thinking about making a similar statement? I know we talked on the trip here—"

Jacob shook his head. "Still flying under the radar, for now."

"Trade." Dane held out the box grater and block of cheese and took the bowl of eggs from Jacob. Letting the sausage simmer, he added dried mustard, salt, and pepper to the eggs and whipped them good. "You're bi, right? Like Bas?"

Jacob nodded.

"I wasn't sure and didn't want to assume," Dane said. "I saw the pictures, saw you flirting with Leah, but then the other night with Julio . . ."

Jacob threw a pinch of shredded cheese at him. "I said don't remind me."

Dane laughed, grabbing the shredded cheese and tossing

161

it into the bowl. He poured heavy cream into it and set it aside. Next, he dumped the sausage mixture onto a paper towel-lined plate and shoved it in the freezer, retrieving the piecrust therefrom.

"Bas isn't mad at you," Dane said, as he poured the egg mixture into the piecrust. "Alex told me the history there. He's angrier at Julio."

"Julio didn't know who I was either."

Dane placed the egg-filled pie on a baking sheet and rested back against the counter. "He knew you were his breaststroke competition. And Bas thinks he knew more." He tapped the tattoo visible below Jacob's short sleeve. "Also how Bas looks at you."

Jacob tugged his sleeve down. "Like a teammate?"

Dane dipped his chin, forcing Jacob to meet his skeptical eyes.

"Bas doesn't want that," Jacob said.

Dane smirked. "You do?"

Jacob stared at his shoes, cheeks heating.

"Don't be so sure you know what Bas wants." Dane pushed off the counter and retrieved the cooled sausage mixture. "I saw how Bas reacted when he found you and Julio together in the lounge that night. He wouldn't have reacted that way over a teammate."

"What are you saying?" Because Jacob wanted to hear it out of someone else's mouth, not just the ramblings of his own imagination.

"You're at the Olympics. If there's ever a time to take a chance, I don't think it'd be wasted." He scattered sausage into the egg pie, like he was scattering water on the seeds of Jacob's hope. "Either way, what happens in Madrid, stays in Madrid. Olympic motto."

"Oh, is that right?" Jacob said, finding himself optimistic for the first time in days. "And how would you know, fellow first timer?"

Dane opened the stove and slid the pie in. "Don't tell anyone," he said in a conspiratorial whisper. "But I'm fucking an expert."

"I think your secret's blown, matey." Jacob tossed a rag at him, both of them laughing.

"I've been meaning to ask," Dane said. "Why the pirate fascination?"

Jacob shrank a little, thinking the pirate thing was another sign of his immaturity, but then Dane clarified. "It's funny as heck. The T-shirts too." He pointed at the one Jacob had thrown on this morning, his favorite faded gray *Dead Men Tell No Tales* one. "I'm just curious. And I have a collection of gaming consoles as far back as the Atari 2600, so you can't out-geek me."

Jacob's breath caught. "You have a 2600?"

"Two, actually. One of the few benefits of having a home-shopping hostess mother." He tossed the rag back at Jacob, hitting him in the chest. "But back to pirates . . ."

Throwing the towel over his shoulder, Jacob flopped into one of the kitchenette chairs. "My dad was a Marine." He fished the dog tags out from under his collar, showing them to Dane. "I'd ask him to tell me about his tours, but they were too . . ."

LAYLA REYNE

He glanced away, swallowing hard, and Dane, lowering into the seat beside him, clasped his forearm. "It's okay, Pup. You don't have to tell me."

Jacob cleared his throat. "No, it's fine. He would spin them into pirate tales instead, appropriate for a kid's ears. It was our thing." He shrugged. "I guess it stuck."

"No wonder you like the water."

Jacob hadn't thought of it that way before, but he had to give it to Dane, maybe it wasn't a coincidence. Maybe he was meant to do this.

Dane twisted in his chair, peering into the oven.

"Speaking of adventures," Jacob said, "what happens with you and Alex, after all this?" He was likewise genuinely curious where the new, high-profile couple went after Madrid.

"I'm moving to Colorado Springs."

"That'll be a change."

"A good one." Dane smiled, then dropped his voice to a whisper again. "There's talk, once Alex's mom gets better, of us moving to LA."

To where Alex had gone to school, to where Bas still lived, to where they'd all swim for the same club. Bas would have all his friends there. Jacob would be an afterthought, again. His hope began to dry up.

Dane nudged his shoulder. "You'll have to come visit us."

Jacob worried a nick in the table. "You guys have your lives, all of you."

"You don't think you're a part of that life now?"

164

"I'm just the kid."

Dane laid a freckled hand over his and waited for Jacob to give him his eyes. When he did, the blue-gray ones staring back at him were warm and bright. "You're family, Jacob. The family I've chosen. I'm not letting you off that easily." Smiling, he lifted a hand and lightly popped Jacob upside the head, as his own mentor Mo was prone to do. "Now get with the program."

BAS SMILED THROUGH the backslaps and handshakes as he strode into the locker room, the gold medal for the two-hundred-meter fly at home around his neck. He was stoked about it, really he was. Another gold to go with his other medals, and he broke his own world record getting it, but his excitement faded each time his thoughts strayed to breakfast.

As he'd approached the lounge, Bas had almost stumbled at the sound of Jacob's laughter. Trailing behind the other guys, no one had seen his misstep or the goofy grin that stretched across his face, so happy to hear Jacob back to his old self. He'd looked it too. Turning the corner into the kitchenette, Bas had seen Jacob smiling and cracking pirate jokes with Dane. But then Jacob had caught sight of him and fumbled through a hasty exit.

According to Dane, Jacob had seemed to be doing better, eager for his race tomorrow, which he'd qualified for in this morning's heat. First place, ahead of Julio. And, when Bas had asked Alex what exactly he'd told Jacob about Julio, Alex claimed to have framed the situation as best he could. Bas had no reason to doubt his best friend. Problem was, there was no good framing it. Bas needed to explain it to Jacob himself, acknowledge that how he'd handled things was wrong, to Jacob and Julio, and clear the air before Jacob's next race. He didn't want to be the one holding Jacob back from gold. That was the opposite of looking out for him and his team.

In front of his open locker, Bas shrugged out of his too-toasty track jacket and dug his phone out of his bag.

Need to talk, he typed in a text to Jacob.

Before Bas hit Send, Julio, dressed in his Team Spain sportswear, sauntered into his row, the Spanish fly swimmer who'd won silver on his heels.

"Amazing run, Stewart," the younger man said. He pushed past Julio, hand outstretched. "Was an honor standing on the podium next to you."

Bas shook his hand. "Thanks, man. You did great too. Congrats."

A stranger would have thought Bas had told him he'd won the lottery, his smile was so big. Both Bas and Julio laughed. Julio tapped the other swimmer's hip. "Go on, Gio. I'll be out in a minute."

Bas straddled the bench and motioned for Julio to also sit. "I'm glad you're here, J. I wanted to talk."

Julio's eyes landed on his chest, on the tattoo of his initials. "You didn't have that four years ago."

No, he hadn't. And Julio had only just gotten the *SS*

tattoo on his right shoulder. Jacob had inked the Spanish rose on his delt a year earlier, but that tattoo hadn't only been about the two of them. It had also been about Julio's Spanish heritage and his time living in California and attending USC. *SS*, however, was clearly about Bas, and those two letters, in stark black ink, in simple serif font, were a commitment that had scared the shit out of then-twenty-two-year-old, commitment-phobic Bas.

He rubbed a hand over his *JE* tattoo. "I got it as a reminder."

"Of me?" Julio looked at him through long dark lashes, not a trace of teasing in his eyes, just all earnest interest. Julio had given him that same look the night he'd pushed up his sleeve and showed off his new ink.

Then Bas had wiped the floor with it, and not in the good way.

Bas snagged his track jacket off the bench and shrugged it back on, zipping it up over the tattoo. "Of me being a dick."

Julio rocked back, eyes wide.

"Look, J, I'm sorry for what happened. I've owed you an apology for years. Leaving you the way I did, it's one of my biggest regrets."

Julio reached out a hand, running it up Bas's thigh. "Sebastian."

Bas laid a hand over his, stilling its motion. "I said *the way* I left, Julio, not *that* I left. That's why I got the tattoo. To remind me of that."

Julio withdrew his hand. "I don't follow."

"We weren't a good fit, Julio. I don't do commitment, it doesn't run in my blood, and you were never going to be comfortable with me being bi. When you went back to Spain, I should have missed you more; that's when I knew it wasn't working. You deserved better, in a relationship, and in the way I ended it. I should have made that call before or after the Olympics, not during, and I sure as hell shouldn't have acted the way I did after. It threw you off your game, and I'm sorry about that, more than you'll ever know."

A minute passed before Julio rose, looming over Bas. "Like Jacob is off his game now?"

Bas hung his head. Julio had read him all right. And knew him too well. "He definitely deserves better."

CHAPTER
FOURTEEN

JACOB HAD DUCKED out of breakfast yesterday morning, mind still a jumbled mess, not sure which path to take. Things had started to thaw between him and Bas after Media Day, and a sprout of hope had broken through the ice with Dane's advice, but the thought of grabbing hold of it was terrifying. Instead, he focused on the things in Dane's words he could grab hold of, confidently. Family and team and swimming. He'd bailed on breakfast, eating a slice of the delicious sausage and egg pie on the way back to his room, then napped while Sean and Kevin were out and the room was quiet. It'd paid off in his heat later that morning. He'd finished first, slated for Lane 5 for tonight's medal race.

Between the heat and now, he'd avoided Bas, avoided Julio, and avoided the scene that Kevin and Sean had tried to bring to their room last night. "Take it to the lounge," he'd told them, and they were happy enough for him not to be mopey that they'd obliged. He'd gone with them for a bit, celebrating their freestyle relay gold, but come time for his nightly call with home, he'd retreated to their room, given his dad his full attention, then taken a long run that knocked him out good. He'd slept through the night for the first time since . . .

He shook off the thought.

None of that.

Blocking out the distraction, he stepped through the holding area door onto the aquatic center deck for his second medal race.

Alex and Coach were waiting for him by the benches. "You ready, kid?" Coach asked.

"Ready, Coach."

"You look good, Pup. Rested," Alex said. He ran his hand over Jacob's head. "And in need of a haircut. Chi-Chi-Chia," he sang, and Jacob batted his hand away, laughing.

"That's what this is for," he said, waving his cap about. He stepped to the pool's edge, splashed water onto himself, and doused the cap and his goggles, snapping them on as he straightened.

"I need to tell you what to do or you got it?" Coach asked.

"I got it," Jacob answered, even as his eyes tracked Tall-Dark-and-Charming sauntering their way.

"Good luck, Burrows." Smirking, Julio walked past them, his tattoos moving as if they were alive. Like Bas was here with them.

Alex stepped in front of Jacob, cutting off his line of sight and patting his cheek. "Focus, Pup."

Jacob blinked fast, forcing the distraction away again.

None of that, he repeated.

Returning his captain's stare, Jacob was focused and

determined.

"There we go," Alex said. "That's what I want to see. Now, send his blimey arse to the bottom of the sea."

The mimicked pirate accent was terrible, but Jacob's chest expanded and warmed for his effort. "Aye, aye, Captain."

Alex tapped his cheek once more, then followed Coach to the bench. The crowd grew louder with each swimmer announced, and Jacob felt good, buoyed by the enthusiasm, as he climbed onto the Lane 5 block and lowered his goggles over his eyes. He shook his limbs loose, ignored the roaring crowd and Julio beside him, and when the call sounded for swimmers to take their marks, he bent in half and gripped the front end of the block.

It was just him and the water for the next two hundred meters. This was the race he swam best. No one could argue that. No one could take that away from him. He just had to claim what he wanted most in this moment. Staring down the lane, what he wanted most was gold.

The horn blew, and unlike the last race, Jacob was ready, his launch textbook, better than. He powered off the block, sliced through the water, and came up farther down the lane than he ever had before. Using the extra power he'd developed in training, the extra rest he'd gotten the past two days, and all the shit that had dogged him as fuel, he cut through the water. He lifted his torso, breathed, and drove his arms forward. Then sinking back in the water, swooped his arms around, pumped his legs, and propelled himself forward.

Over and over.

Four laps, legs, arms, and lungs burning.

Just him and the narrow strip of water between the ropes. No distractions.

His fingers slammed the wall at the end of the last fifty meters, and he heaved out of the water, gasping. Ripping off his cap and goggles, he splashed around in the lane and looked up at the leaderboard.

1. J. Burrows, USA

And to the right of his time, the fastest he'd ever clocked, *OR/WR.*

Frozen in shock, the next thing he knew, Alex and Coach were hoisting him out of the pool and into a back-pounding hug.

"You did it, Jacob!" Alex shouted over the roaring crowd. "Fucking smashed the Olympic and world records!"

"Amazing job, kid!" Coach cheered, his normally stern face awkwardly painted with a huge smile. "Another medal, Burrows. Great first outing."

The other swimmers from his race slapped his back and offered congrats as they passed, including Julio, who'd come in second.

"Go take the post-race test and put on your track jacket," Alex said. "It's time to stand on top of the fucking podium!"

Finally! He was back on track, feeling like himself again, like he hadn't let his team and family down. Just inside the tunnel, Dane, on his way out for the next event, met him with open arms. Jacob ran into them.

"Now that's what I'm talking about," Dane said, lifting him off his feet.

When Dane put him back down, Jacob held out a fist. "Your turn."

"You know it." Dane bumped back, top and bottom, put on his real smile, and stepped out of the tunnel. The crowd went wild, and Jacob liked to think maybe he'd had something to do with pumping them up. Dane jabbed the air with his fist, high-fived Coach when he reached the blocks, and pulled his captain boyfriend into another pre-race kiss.

The crowd noise was deafening, so loud Jacob almost missed the voice behind him. "Fucking great swim, Pup."

Spinning around, Jacob spotted Bas, shoulder leaning against the wall of the tunnel. He hadn't realized how much he'd wanted Bas here to celebrate with him until he saw him standing there. "Yeah, it was. I won a freaking gold medal." He was about to step forward, make his move, because what else was he supposed to do with all this happiness and hope, when Bas held out his phone.

"We thought it was going to blow up the locker."

Drying his hands on the towel over his shoulder, Jacob took the phone from Bas and unlocked it. His screen filled with texts and social-media alerts, so many of them in shouty caps. He opened the text from Josh first and dropped the phone.

By his side, Bas saved it from the concrete floor. "Hey, what's wrong?"

Jacob shook his head, swallowing around the knot in his throat. With trembling hands, he took the phone back and opened the text again, turning the screen so Bas could see the picture of Josh and his dad. They were holding a US flag and smiling like they'd won the lottery. "That's the biggest I've seen Dad smile since he came back from Afghanistan. I never thought . . ." He lost his words again, only finding them when Bas cradled his cheek. "I never thought I'd see him happy like that again."

"That's a good thing, Jacob. *You* did a good thing."

"Yeah, it is. I did that," he forced out around a riot of senses and emotions.

Happiness and relief.

Bas's warm hand on his cheek, his blue eyes inviting.

Hope.

There was only one place for all that to go. Time to grab hold. He checked quickly that the tunnel was deserted, then launched at Bas, slamming him back against the wall and capturing his lips.

Wind knocked out of him, Bas huffed a breath against Jacob's lips, startled, but with his next breath, he groaned and lifted his other hand, framing Jacob's face and giving in to the kiss, tongue tracing Jacob's lips, asking for entrance. Jacob granted it, opening for Bas and diving in himself. He pressed closer, wanting to feel Bas's body again, thrilling when he found it hard in all the right places. Bracing his forearm against the wall, Jacob trailed his other hand over Bas's race-shaven jaw, down his corded neck, and across his smooth chest, coming to rest over his pounding heart.

The next second, Bas was gone, tearing his lips and body away. Jacob nearly face-planted into the wall. Catching himself with both hands, he spun around.

Wide-eyed, chest heaving, and definitely turned on, Bas was holding himself back against the opposite wall. "What are you doing?"

Jacob crossed the tunnel, closing the distance between them again. "Another good thing."

Bas slipped out from in front of him, striding a few steps down the tunnel. "This is not a good thing."

"Why the hell not?" Jacob braced a hand against the wall, hope and happiness fleeting, doubt and confusion rushing back in. But with anger joining this time. "I don't understand. We were together in Vienna, and then you were gone. You said one night, so I forced myself to let it go. You tried to patch things up with me and Leah, but then you were pissed when I flirted with Julio. And now you kiss me like that and say it's a *bad* thing. I'm confused, Bas."

"That's right," Bas said. "You're confused. You're nineteen, Pup. You don't know what you really want. Leah, Julio, me: make a choice."

Jacob shoved off the wall. "You're a choice?"

"No," Bas snapped, taking a step back from him.

"The only reason I gave Leah or Julio a second look was because you took yourself out of the running. I want you!"

"You don't know what you really want."

Stumbling like he'd been hit in the stomach, Jacob scrabbled at the wall to keep from falling. "Are you seriously throwing that back in my face? After what you said to me that night in Vienna."

"Shit, Jacob, I'm sorry. That's not what I meant." His eyes were as tossed and tortured as Jacob's insides. He stepped forward, then rocked to a halt, hand rubbing his chest. Right over the tattoo. "Trust me, *I'm* not what you want. I'm no good for you."

Not giving Jacob a chance to argue, Bas turned and stalked away, down the tunnel toward the exit. Jacob's legs and heart were too weak to follow. Leaning back against the wall, he closed his eyes and struggled to breathe. He'd been about to cry with joy five minutes ago, and now he was on the verge of tears for an entirely different reason.

"Burrows."

Jacob shook his head against the wall. "I can't deal with you right now."

Julio kept coming, footsteps growing louder as he approached. "It's not about you; it's about him. And me."

Jacob righted his gaze. "What's that supposed to mean?"

"He regrets leaving me." Julio tapped his chest, right where his initials were inked on Bas's skin. Over his heart. Where Bas couldn't seem to stop rubbing his hand. "His biggest regret. He told me that yesterday."

Julio's implication was clear. Bas regretted leaving him and wanted him back. It sure as hell made more sense than Bas wanting Jacob. Tall, dark, and handsome Julio was older, cooler, charming. Not a nineteen-year-old virgin dork with fucked-up hair and crooked teeth who spouted pirate quips and couldn't be depended on to win. And while Bas questioned that Jacob knew what he wanted, there was no question what Julio wanted. He already had Bas's initials inked on his shoulder.

But something didn't fit. "Bas started pulling away before we even got here," Jacob said.

"Because I messaged him in advance." One corner of Julio's mouth kicked up. "Told him I wanted to see him. That I wanted to patch things up."

Phone clattering to the ground, Jacob clutched at the wall with both hands to hold himself up.

"Cut your losses now, Burrows," Julio said. "You got two medals out of this. More than most people can say."

"The medley relay, though . . ."

"You think you can handle that? You choked your first race. Yeah, you won this one, but that just proves you're running hot and cold. What's it gonna be at the medley relay? That gold means everything to them. You want to disappoint them? To cost them the most important race here? Of their careers? The last race they may ever swim?"

No, no, he didn't. Not even his heartache and anger would justify risking what Dane, Alex, and Bas and the rest of the team had worked so hard for.

As he stood on the medal stand twenty minutes later, Jacob hoped the spectators here, his father and family watching the live stream back home, and the millions of other viewers mistook his mournful tears for joy.

DREADS LOOSE AND dripping wet, track suit sticking to his damp skin, Bas scaled the dorm stairs three at a time, Alex on his heels. They burst through the stairwell door onto the second floor, drawing more than a few startled looks as they ran down the hall to the triple.

"Do you have any idea what's going on?" Alex asked.

"You think my answer's changed in the past hour?"

His answer—*I don't know*—was ninety percent a lie. Bas was fairly certain Jacob's no-show at the medley relay heat this morning had to do with their kiss and argument yesterday after Jacob's medal race. The ten percent he actually didn't know was if the last-minute text Jacob had sent Terrence, claiming to be sick, was true. He doubted it. Jacob hadn't seemed the least bit sick last night. Even taking Bas's idiocy yesterday into account, he was surprised Jacob had missed today's heat. Unless he really was sick. Hungover, maybe? He wouldn't need to use that fake ID here to get a bottle of Cuervo.

Outside Jacob's door, Bas raised his first to knock, but Alex grabbed his biceps first, hauling him around. "What the fuck happened?"

Bas wrenched his arm free and pounded on the door. "Jacob, open up!"

The door swung open, but it wasn't the swimmer Bas wanted to see. "Dude," Kevin said. "What's going on?"

Alex crowded into the doorway next to Bas. "Where's your roommate?"

Sean appeared behind Kevin. "Right here?"

"The other one," Bas said, pushing into the room. He knew which bed was Jacob's on first glance. Military neat, like Jacob had kept it when they'd shared a room. Bas put a hand to the sheets. Cold. Had the bed been that cold and neat all night?

He straightened, turning back around to Kevin and Sean. "When's the last time you saw Jacob?"

"What the hell's going on?" Sean asked.

"Jacob didn't show for the medley relay heat," Alex answered.

"Oh shit," Kevin cursed. "Did you guys still qualify?"

"Yes," Bas grit out. Terrence had subbed in and done the best he could, but he didn't have Jacob's speed or hours of practice in the lineup. "Back to my question. When's the last time you saw the pup?"

Sean bowed his head, hand scrubbing the nape of his neck. "Yesterday."

"He didn't sleep here last night?" Alex clipped in his captain-voice.

"He wasn't here when we got in, and he wasn't here this morning."

"And you didn't think to tell someone?" Bas roared.

"Dude," Kevin shouted back, stepping to Sean's defense. "We thought he was with you!"

No, he most definitely was not. Bas had made sure of that. Now *no one* knew where Jacob was. Gone overnight, in a strange city, and he'd missed his call time this morning. Because Bas had been a fucking idiot. He'd done it again. Just like four years ago. Jeopardized his team and hurt the man he lo—

"Fuck!" He swiped an arm across Jacob's bedside table, sending his alarm clock and medals crashing to the floor.

Along with Davis's dog tags.

They tumbled end over end, to the middle of the floor, landing in a ray of sun and reflecting the harsh midday light at Bas.

Wherever Jacob was, he hadn't taken the tags with him.

He wasn't safe.

Sean bent to pick them up.

"Don't!" Bas snapped.

Retracting his hand, Sean backed off. "Look, man, he's our teammate and friend too. How can we help?"

"Go get Dane," Alex ordered Sean. "He was a few minutes behind us, wrapping up with the press. Tell him to bring his computer."

"Burrows!" Coach's voice boomed down the hallway.

"You." Alex pointed at Kevin, as he kicked the items Bas had scattered on the floor under the bed. "In the bathroom and make puking noises. We told Coach that Jacob was sick."

Kevin jumped to it, closing the bathroom door behind him, just as Coach came through the other one. "Where's Burrows? I saw Sean running out."

On cue, Kevin made retching noises, and Alex eyed the closed bathroom door.

Coach grimaced. "Does he need to go to medical?"

Alex shook his head. "Ate something bad after his race last night. Can't be much left at this point."

More retching noises from the bathroom, and Coach stepped back toward the hallway. "Get food and fluids in him. If he can't keep it down, get him to medical for an IV. I want him ready for tomorrow tonight. We're not losing that gold."

"Yes, Coach," Alex said.

Once Hartl was gone, Bas grabbed Alex by the arm. "Why didn't you tell him the truth? Jacob's missing. We need help finding him."

"If Coach or the Committee finds out he was an intentional no-show, they won't let him swim tomorrow. Do you want that?"

Fuck no, he didn't want that. He didn't want any of this. He wanted Jacob to have his shot at relay gold, along with the rest of his squad. But finding Jacob, making sure he was safe, had to be paramount. "How are we going to find him?"

"I'm going to track his phone," Dane said from the doorway, laptop under his arm. "He's always got it on him, yeah?"

Bas nodded. Jacob never went anywhere without that phone, in case his dad or Josh needed to reach him.

Kneeling, Bas retrieved the dog tags and medals from under the bed. He set the medals back on the table and clutched the tags in his hand.

Dane set up on Jacob's bed, hacker face on and laptop open, while Alex checked the hallway to make sure Coach was gone, before ushering Sean and Kevin out too.

Pacing, Bas flipped the tags over in his hand, like he'd seen Jacob do so many times. First, Jacob had told him his dad had given him these for luck. Then, that night at Martin's, he'd revealed his dad had meant them as a token of safety. That was what Bas had thought he was doing. Keeping Jacob safe, watching out for him, while Jacob watched out for everyone else.

Bang-up job Bas had done there. He cursed himself as every worst-case scenario ran through his head. Jacob in a strange city, alone, overnight. Jacob hiding from him, from the team, thinking they didn't need him. Jacob in someone else's room—Julio's maybe. That was the worst-case scenario of all, making Bas want to retch for real.

Alex's sharp tone jolted him out of the spiral. "All right, cut the bullshit. Tell me what happened."

"We had a . . . disagreement . . . after his race yesterday."

"He made a move, didn't he?" Dane said, his fingers not pausing in their sprint across the keyboard. "I encouraged him. It's not all Bas's fault."

Alex's dark eyes remain locked on Bas. "I asked if you knew what you were doing. Multiple times."

Sinking onto the end of Jacob's bed, Bas braced his elbows on his knees and hung his head in his hands, hiding behind his dreads. "Clearly I didn't."

He could feel Alex's hard stare on the back of his head. "Is this about Espo?" When Bas didn't respond, Alex knelt in front of him and dipped his head, forcing his gaze. "I'm asking as your friend, Sebastian, not your captain."

Bas dropped his hands, letting them dangle between his knees, tags swinging by their chain. "I was trying to do right by him."

"Julio?" Dane said.

"Fuck no," Bas said over his shoulder. "That's done. I told Julio as much the other day."

"Good," Dane replied, and Bas looked back to Alex, who was giving him the spill-it stare.

"You're not totally wrong," Bas conceded. "This is about Julio. I don't want to hurt Jacob the way I hurt him."

"By leaving him?" Alex said.

Bas cast his gaze aside, out the window.

"How do you know you'll leave?" Alex said.

"I don't do commitment."

"More bullshit." The certainty in Alex's voice had Bas whipping his gaze back around.

"How so? Julio is the only serious relationship I've had, and I left him when he needed me most. Jacob asked me to stay, and I left him too."

"That doesn't mean you don't do commitment," Alex said. "You've stayed by my grumpy side for how long?"

"Because you're my best friend."

Standing, Alex rested back against the windowsill. "You don't think Jacob could be that person too?"

"You can have more than one," Dane interjected.

"You're a mentor at your club," Alex talked over him. "You run a tattoo parlor. You make it to your mom's house every weekend."

"And I'm supposed to add a relationship to that?"

"You haven't already?"

In his head, Bas rewound the past month between him and Jacob—the friendship, the closeness, the caring, the desire, the sex. Alex's question was a fair one. Bas knew the answer, as sure as Alex did. He was falling for Jacob, fast. The beautiful, strong, observant young man who'd been a constant in his life this summer, no matter how hard Bas had tried to push him away.

And just look at how he'd hurt Jacob already. Would hurt him more.

"Even if he'd have me," Bas said, "I can't give this a shot, then leave him. He's already lost too much." His mother who'd deserted him, the dates who didn't get his bisexuality, and fuck all else who'd written chapters of Jacob's story that had the protagonist looking out for himself last.

Bas had to put Jacob first. Change the story.

Stay away from him and stay away from breaking both their hearts.

But damn if it didn't feel like his heart was breaking now anyway . . .

"Why are you so sure you'll leave?" Alex asked.

"Three generations—my father, grandfather, great-grandfather—they all cheated and left. I don't want to be the fourth. If I never—"

"Did you cheat on Julio, before you broke it off?" Dane asked.

"No, of course not."

"That right there," Alex said, jabbing a finger at him. "That's why you're not like the other men in your family. Your *mother* raised you, she never deserted you, and you haven't deserted her either. Fuck the other half of your DNA."

Even if Alex was right . . . "I don't know how to do this." He spread his hands, a poor encapsulation of their current predicament, but there it was. "Look at the mess I made of things. I haven't had a relationship since Julio. Four years, I've kept hookups casual so I wouldn't fuck up again, exactly like this. *Christ,* how much have I hurt him already?"

Alex was quiet a moment, then pushed off the window-sill. Sitting next to Bas, he folded his fingers around the tags and slipped them out of Bas's grasp. "Are you really afraid of leaving Jacob? Or are you more afraid of Jacob leaving you?"

The notion made every muscle in Bas's body tighten, including the one at the center of his chest. Jacob's kindness, his smile, his kiss, his earnestness that had filled Bas's life, one day ripped away. Bas's dad had been thirty-five when he'd left, a grown-up who was supposed to have known what we wanted. He'd changed his mind, leaving Bas and his mom behind. Jacob was so young; he still had so many choices to make. "He's only nineteen."

"The oldest nineteen-year-old any of us have ever met."

"He hasn't had much experience. He's going to want to explore."

"Is that why you broke up with Julio?" Dane asked. "Because you wanted to explore?"

"No," Bas answered without hesitation. "We were both young, immature, and besides swimming, we didn't have much else in common. He didn't like that I was bi either, and with him going back to Spain, and me in California, we'd already started growing apart, even though we tried to ignore it."

"The real reason, Sebastian," Alex prompted.

Bas rewound his thoughts and words, putting it together. Alex was right. *He* didn't want to be the one left behind on the shower floor crying, heart ripped out and future uncertain. "I'm afraid of him leaving me."

Alex nodded. "You're scared; not that those other reasons you and Julio didn't work out weren't valid too."

"Even so," Dane said, "do you regret the two years you spent with Julio?"

"No, never. I cared about him. I regret how I ended it, not that it ended."

"Then why won't you give Jacob a shot too? Even if it doesn't work out, do you want to pass up the chance? Because you're afraid of what *might* happen in the future?"

"Honestly, Bas," Alex said, "he's more likely to lose you—or you him—in a car accident tomorrow than either one of you is to leave, from what I've seen of you two together. You're like fucking magnets, always gravitating toward each other. The fact you're fighting this hard to stay apart should tell you something. Maybe you should just be together."

There was a tablet full of drawings in Bas's room proving Alex's point. Jacob was always on his mind. He couldn't get him out of his head, or his heart. He just had to take a leap. Like he had opening the tattoo shop, which had been a success. Like he had giving Dane the benefit of the doubt when he'd chased after Alex, which had been a success. Could he and Jacob be a success too? Could they make it work? Could his heart afford not to try?

Could Jacob's?

Jacob, who'd put himself first for a change, who'd asked Bas for a chance, who'd asked him to stay and change his story.

Had Bas been writing it wrong? Could he write a happily ever after for him and Jacob instead?

"I got him," Dane said behind them, and both Alex and Bas shot off the bed. "Plaza Mayor."

The very center of the city. In the middle of the day. Between the work crush and the tourist crush, it'd be like hunting a needle in a haystack. "How precise is whatever you're doing?" Bas asked.

Dane glanced up, one side of his mouth hitched. "Right now, looks like he's sitting at the base of the light post to the right of the horse's ass. Precise enough for you?"

In more ways than one. "I need to go," Bas said, holding his hand out to Alex, palm up.

Alex dropped the dog tags in his hand. "Suspect that you do."

Bas looped the tags over his neck, tucking them under his shirt, and with the rubber band on his wrist, tied his dreads up high. Go time. "Text me if his location changes," he said to Dane. Then to Alex, "Cover for us if we're late getting back."

"Not too late," Alex said, opening the door for him. "You've got a medal race to win tonight. And we've got the big one tomorrow."

Only Jacob's words would do. "Aye, aye, Captain."

BALL CAP PULLED low, knees tucked to his chest, Jacob made himself as small as possible, out of the way of the tourists and locals crowding the historic Madrid square. The blazing midday sun did nothing to scare away the horde of people. Used to the Texas heat, it didn't scare away Jacob either. The trails of sweat running down his temples and back felt like home. The colorful umbrellas at the outdoor cafés lining the square also reminded him of San Antonio. He could have gone into one, rested indoors after a night outside wandering the city, but he had zero appetite, the thought of food making him nauseous.

Besides, out here in the packed Plaza Mayor, he could get lost. Dressed in cargo shorts and a T-shirt, with his faded Longhorns hat shadowing his face, no one gave him a second look. Just another American tourist in Madrid for the Games. He wasn't instantly recognizable like Dane, a familiar face like Alex, or a towering tattooed man with dreadlocks like Bas.

Thinking of the latter made his stomach churn. He was usually so good at reading people, reading situations, but he'd read this one all wrong. He laid his head on his knees and closed his eyes, retreating from the light. Behind his eyelids, the Not-Top-Ten reel that had been plaguing him all night continued to play.

Caught jerking off in San Antonio.

Two embarrassing breakdowns in Vienna.

The room reassignment in Madrid.

Flirting with Bas's ex opening night.

Faltering in his hundred-meter race.

Winning the two hundred, going after what he wanted, and being told he didn't know what he wanted.

Jacob seeing something more between him and Bas than was there.

Julio overhearing their argument.

Julio, who was at the top of Bas's regrets list.

Missing the medley relay heat this morning.

His team hadn't needed him for that last one. They'd gone ahead without him, Terrence swimming his breast-stroke laps. He'd checked the standings on his phone; they'd qualified. Not as fast as they'd been swimming with Jacob in the lineup, but the unexpected change likely had shaken them up. They'd work it out by tomorrow, and with as up and down as Jacob had been, Terrence was a safer bet. Bas wouldn't have to worry about Terrence—personally or professionally. Terrence wouldn't cost them their gold.

His phone vibrated for the umpteenth time the past hour. By now, his teammates had figured out he hadn't come back to the Village last night and were frantically calling and texting. None from Bas, however. Jacob needed to call Alex, tell him he was okay and apologize for missing the heat. Tell him that Terrence should swim in the final tomorrow. Jacob wasn't ready for that conversation yet. He checked each text, just in case it was Coach. No word from him yet either, which Jacob assumed meant the team was covering for him. He needed to thank Alex for that too. He also checked each text in case one was from Josh or his dad. It would be off schedule, early morning in Texas, but they'd called earlier another time this week.

Which they were doing so again today, his dad's face filling the screen. Jacob answered, bringing the phone to his ear. "Hey, Dad, how's it going?"

"Good, good. I took the whole weekend off to watch you swim."

Jacob reached into his pocket for the dog tags and felt doubly bereft at finding his pocket empty, realizing he'd left the tags in his room. God, how much had he lost in the past twenty-four hours?

"Jacob, you there?"

He cleared his throat. "Yeah, sorry, Dad, just loud out here."

"Where's that?"

"I'm in the Plaza Mayor."

"The Plaza what?"

"The big town square in Madrid." He switched on the camera and flipped the phone around, angling it slightly up and moving it left to right so his dad could see the buildings on the square.

Davis whistled low, and Jacob turned the phone back around to see him smiling wistfully. "They sure do build 'em beautiful over there."

"Were you ever here?" He rarely asked specifics about his dad's time in the Marines, the fictionalized story time almost more than he'd wanted to risk, worried about triggering a flashback. But today, on screen, his father looked calm and happy to reminisce.

"No, the base is farther south, near Seville, but the architecture is similar. Unit only got to stay there a week while we resupplied, but it sure was beautiful. And hot."

"The hot part's not changed," Jacob said, taking comfort in his dad's answering laugh and upbeat demeanor. "You look good, Dad."

"Thanks, and don't take this the wrong way, kid, but you don't. You gonna be ready for tomorrow? Everyone's coming over for the main event."

Which he wouldn't be swimming in anymore. Guilt walloped him, making him rock in place. He didn't have the heart to tell his dad the truth, not when he looked so happy. Jacob switched off the camera before his dad could read the truth on his face, bringing the phone back to his ear. "You did tell them it's not a boxing match, right?" he joked.

"Of course I did. We all want to see you swim."

"I haven't been swimming so great."

"Are you kidding me? You've got two Olympic medals."

"One bronze."

"You've got two, kid, and one of 'em's gold. More than

most people. And you're only nineteen. You'll get the gold in all the events next time."

That might be true, if he were even allowed back after the no-show this morning. Regardless of *his* chances for a repeat, this was likely it for Alex, Dane, and Bas. "There might not be a next time for some of my teammates."

"Let them worry about that."

As much as Jacob wished he could, that wasn't him. He'd always feel responsible, and if he cost his team the medley relay gold they'd lost last time, that guilt would surely knock him all the way over. He couldn't let them risk the gold on him.

"So, what's got you in such a good mood, besides the weekend off?" he asked his father, deflecting, but also curious.

"You'll never believe who and what rolled into the shop yesterday."

"I got nothing. Tell me."

"Sixty-four and half, cherry red Mustang convertible. With Darlene Harris behind the wheel."

"Mona Harris's daughter?" Jacob asked. "You went to school with Darlene, didn't you?" She'd been his dad's prom date, if Jacob remembered the old yearbooks correctly.

"That's her. She's a nurse and moved back to help take care of Mona. She's divorced. Got a boy and girl too, high schoolers. Fans of yours. I invited them over to watch tomorrow night."

More people he'd disappoint. He rested his head back on his knees, eyes closed, as he swallowed around the lump in his throat.

His dad broke the silence, voice laden with concern. "Jacob, buddy, tell me what's going on."

Tears burned his eyes. "I screwed up, Dad. Everything's a mess, and I'm afraid I've disappointed everyone."

"You haven't."

The words hadn't come from his dad on the phone. They'd come from above, in a deep voice Jacob had wanted to hear more than any other, even if the prospect of what might follow scared the hell out of him. He thought maybe he was hearing things, until a rough hand landed on his shin and a waft of chlorine floated under his nose.

He opened his eyes.

Bas was kneeling in front of him, blue eyes warm and relieved. When he spoke, his words were soft yet firm. Certain. "You could never disappoint anyone."

CHAPTER
SIXTEEN

BAS HADN'T KNOWN it was possible for a heart to soar and crash at the same time. Not until he pushed through the plaza crowd and saw a raggedy-ass orange baseball cap resting atop knobby knees. Jacob was safe, right where Dane said he would be.

Pure relief.

But that long rangy body Bas had come to appreciate and want was curled in on itself, all of Jacob's limbs tucked in tight like an injured animal hiding from the world.

Pure regret.

Bas had done that to him.

This was not a page in the pup's story he'd wanted to write. Fuck, he'd wanted to tear out all the pages like this and burn them, set fire and banish all the people and events that had caused Jacob pain. Instead, he'd added to them. He'd thought he'd been protecting Jacob by pushing him away. All he'd done instead was hurt him. Like he'd hurt Julio, only worse. Because Jacob shared none of the blame here. Because this could have been so much more. And fuck if Bas didn't still want that. He wanted Jacob—caring, perceptive, funny, open, beautiful, pirate-quoting dork that he was. But how could he convince Jacob he'd cherish all he had to offer when Bas had so miserably failed to do so up to this point?

Rectifying his mistakes would have to wait, though. Bas had to put Jacob's needs first, which most urgently included getting him back to Olympic Village and rested for tomorrow's race. Bas would not let gold slip through the squad's fingers because of his idiocy.

As he approached, he noticed a phone to Jacob's ear and heard him say "Dad." He went on to say that he'd messed up and was afraid he'd disappointed everyone. Nothing could be further from the truth.

"You haven't," Bas said, standing above him.

Jacob jolted but didn't look up. Kneeling, Bas reached out a hand, slow like he'd seen Jacob do, and placed it on Jacob's shin. Jacob opened his eyes, and the tears threatening there shattered Bas's heart where it lay at the younger man's feet.

"You could never disappointment anyone," he assured him.

Jacob just stared, unblinking, as his father's shouts from the phone grew increasingly frantic. Slipping the phone from Jacob's hand, Bas flipped on the camera and waved at Davis Burrows.

"Hey, Mr. B.," he said lightly, pretending like his world wasn't also falling apart. "I snagged the phone from your son so I could say hi in person."

Davis calmed, the lines on his forehead smoothing out

beneath a headful of shaggy blond hair like his son's, pre-buzz cut. "Sebastian, right?"

"Yes, sir. Pleasure to meet you."

"Same to you. Listen, my boy's worried about the race tomorrow."

Bas shifted to sit next to Jacob, throwing an arm over his shoulders so they were both in the camera's view. "He's got nothing to worry about. We're going to win, and Jacob's going to add another gold to his collection."

"Good," Davis said. "Get that through his thick skull, won't you? He's stubborn sometimes, like his old man."

Bas chuckled, pulling a stiff Jacob closer. "I'll try, sir."

"You ever in San Antonio, Sebastian, you come by."

"I'd like that."

Davis's gaze shifted to Jacob, and his smile dimmed, concerned for his son. "Jacob, you gonna win tomorrow?"

When Jacob didn't answer, Bas gave him a shake, whispering in his ear, "Your dad needs to know you're okay."

Arm around his shoulders, Bas felt Jacob summon up the mask, his spine straightening as he inhaled a deep breath. "Yeah, we're going to win, Dad."

"All right, then. It looks hot there. I'll let you boys go. Medal or not, we're proud of you."

"Thanks, Mr. B.," Bas said, passing the phone back to Jacob.

Father and son exchanged a few parting words before ending the call. Jacob pocketed the phone, glancing sideways. "Why did you tell him I was going to win the gold tomorrow?"

"Because you are."

Jacob shifted out from under his arm. "What are you doing here?"

"I'm here for you."

"You don't want me." Jacob paused, then added, "On your team."

By the tears welling in his eyes, Jacob clearly believed both to be true.

Both were dead wrong, and Bas intended to set the record straight, once he got Jacob back to safety. He curled a hand over Jacob's knee. "Can I take you back to the Village, please?"

"I'm fine here."

"Well, I'm not leaving you here, and while you can disguise yourself, I can't." Over Jacob's shoulder, he'd spotted someone with a camera aimed straight at them. He needed to get them out of here. He stood, hand outstretched. "Come on, Jacob," he said, using the direct address he knew Jacob liked.

It worked, if begrudgingly, Jacob glaring as he took his hand. Once standing, he tried to pull free, but Bas didn't let him go. He wasn't going to lose him again, not in the crowd and not until he apologized.

Their trip back to Olympic Village couldn't have been more different than their last cab ride together, when Jacob's face had been buried in Bas's neck. Now, Jacob sat as far away as possible in the back seat, dozing against the opposite window, while Bas texted Alex updates.

I found him. We're on our way back. Where's Coach? Given the earlier story they'd fed Coach, Bas needed to get Jacob inside without being seen.

Pool. You need backup?

Later, maybe, when I go to swim. Bas had his last individual race tonight, the evening's final event, but that swim was hours away. He had a heart to win first.

I'll send Dane.

Thanks.

Good luck.

He darkened the screen just as they turned toward Olympic Village. Leaning forward, Bas directed the driver to the closest drop-off for their building. He shoved a wad of Euros at him and followed Jacob out. Inside, it was quiet in the lobby and on the second floor, most of the athletes at events or lunch. When Jacob stopped in front of the door to his triple, Bas pressed a hand to his back and redirected him across the hall.

"We need to talk," he said, cutting off Jacob's protest.

He unlocked his door and nudged Jacob inside. Windows open, a warm breeze wafted in and sunlight slanted across the two twin beds Bas had pushed together in the center of the room.

Shoulders slumped, Jacob stopped in the entryway, just past the bathroom. "I'm sorry I missed the heat this morning."

"Jesus, Jacob, you're not the one who needs to apologize."

"I read this wrong." He turned toward the door. "You don't owe me—"

"Yeah, I do," Bas said, blocking his exit. Slowly, he raised a hand and cupped Jacob's cheek, the overnight scruff lighting his blood on fire. "I owe you an apology and so much more."

Jacob looked up at him, the midday sun making his green eyes glow, and Bas wanted nothing more than to slide his hand around the back of Jacob's neck, draw him in, and kiss away all of his doubts. But that would be doing what Bas wanted, not what Jacob needed, especially when those same eyes were filled with resignation and hurt. Jacob needed an explanation and reassurance that he was wanted and needed, on the team and by Bas. He deserved to know none of this was on him.

Hand at Jacob's back, Bas led him into the bathroom, lowered the toilet lid, and turned Jacob around. "Sit," he said, and waited for the younger man to get situated before stepping between his thighs. Bas removed his ball cap, tossed it on the vanity, and ran a hand over his head, over the blond Chia Pet fuzz.

"We need to fix this," he said. By Jacob's sharp inhale, he'd caught the double meaning. Stepping back, Bas wet a washcloth in the sink and held it out to Jacob with a dry towel. "Wipe down while I grab the clippers out of my bag."

Jacob took the rags from Bas, fingers brushing his, heat flaring at the connection. Bas forced himself to retreat, to gather himself and the things he needed. He couldn't screw this up. Jacob, his team, their future depended on it. He dug through his bag on the luggage rack below the window, and collected his clippers. He started back for the bathroom, before remembering what else he needed to make his case.

His tablet lay facedown on the bed where he'd tossed it this morning. He always spoke best through this artwork. It was one of the tells Julio had picked up on, together with the way Jacob and Bas watched and gravitated toward each other. The tattoo on Jacob's outer shoulder, inked after only a week and a half of knowing him, was some of Bas's best work. Simple, yet his admiration and affection for Jacob were right there to see for anyone who knew what to look for, especially Julio. Bas should have recognized it earlier himself; some part of him had, the truth too stark to deny. He'd fought like hell to ignore those feelings, then pushed Jacob away to avoid acting on them. He prayed he hadn't lost everything, most of all Jacob, in the process.

Bas carried the clippers and tablet back into the bathroom. Exhausted, Jacob, who'd removed his shirt, wiped down, and slung the dry towel over his bare shoulders, wavered where he sat, head bobbing. Bas considered telling him to go lie down. They could talk later, after Bas's race and after Jacob had rested, but then Jacob's eyes fluttered open, slices of green looking up at him through burnished-gold lashes.

"Fix it," he invited, his double meaning just as clear as Bas's earlier declaration.

Bas set the tablet aside, within reach, and stepped between Jacob's legs again, flipping the clippers on. Blade to scalp, he ran it over Jacob's head in long sweeps, same as he'd done two weeks ago.

"I'm sorry," Bas said after several passes. "For what I said yesterday after your race."

Jacob tried to tip his head up. "You don't have to—"

"I do." Bas grasped his chin and held him level. "Of all people, I understand what it means to be bisexual, and I understand what it means to be doubted because of it. It's one of the reasons Julio and I would never have worked, long-term. I don't want you to ever think I'm doubting you, your choices, or throwing that in your face. And I'll never expect you to make a choice between men or women, or doubt you because you like both. It's who you are. End of story." He made two more passes with the clippers. "And I wouldn't want you any other way."

Jacob's pulse kicked under his fingers. "'Want'? You've been acting like I'm the last person you want."

"*Acting*, because I'm an idiot." He tipped back Jacob's face. "Nothing could be further from the truth." He thought back to his conversation with Leah. All those things she liked about Jacob were the reasons Bas liked him too. More than liked, as he'd all but confessed to his mother. But just as he'd told Leah, Jacob was the one who deserved to hear the praise. Needed to hear it. "You're an amazing swimmer, Jacob. Not to mention smart, funny, perceptive, and beautiful."

"Beautiful." Jacob's chuckle was colored with doubt. "More like an uncoordinated mess of limbs."

"That too, but no less beautiful for it. I want you, baby, and I'm sorry I made you think otherwise. Truth is, that night at the tattoo parlor ruined me for anybody else."

"How can I believe—"

"I have no right to ask you to," Bas conceded. "But let

me show you my truth." He turned off the clippers, reached for his tablet, and handed it to Jacob. "Open the DPR folder."

"'DPR'?" Jacob asked, as he tapped the folder on the screen.

"Dread Pirate Roberts."

Jacob's soft chuckle turned to a gasp as he opened the first of countless sketches. Not of tattoos but of him. A whole folder full of them, of his muse. Jacob's face, his profile, his body in motion, in the pool and in ecstasy.

Jacob's eyes grew wider with each image, his cheeks flaming bright red at the one Bas had drawn after their night together in Vienna. Jacob asleep in the moonlight, Bas having sat up to watch him. Jacob ran his fingers over the lines of his parted lips, his muscled back, his smooth bare hip, digitally smudging them. Bas didn't object. These were as much Jacob's drawings as they were his. When Jacob reached the last one—his pained face from after the race last night, a nightmare image that had kept Bas awake until he'd drawn it out—he peered at it a long minute, before closing the tablet and handing it back to Bas. "Why did you push me away?"

Bas set the tablet on the vanity and clicked the clippers on again. He swiped over Jacob's scalp with his hand, feeling for the natural fade, and Jacob shivered, bracing a hand on Bas's thigh. It damn near burned him, but Bas pushed on, owing Jacob an answer. "At first I thought I was protecting you and the team."

"Because of what happened at the last Olympics?"

"I didn't want to cost the team gold after I made such a mess of things last time." He started on the right side fade. "And I didn't want to hurt you. The men in my family are not the best at being faithful. They cheat and leave. And I've played the field, all sides. A medley of bedmates . . ."

Jacob squeezed his thigh. "Now *you're* internalizing the stereotype. That has nothing to do with you being bi."

Fuck, this kid was so much smarter than any of them gave him credit for. Smiling softly, Bas moved on to the left side. "You're right. It had everything to do with me being a scared idiot. It was an excuse. I'm afraid because I don't know how much longer *you're* going to want *me*."

"You just said my bisexuality didn't make you doubt."

"It doesn't. Your age does."

Jacob's hand shot off his thigh, darting up and wrapping around his hand, halting Bas from taking another pass with the clippers. "I'm old enough to know what I want." His voice was stronger than it'd been all afternoon, some of the fire back in it.

"For how long?"

Jacob gentled his grip, a caress almost. "Bas—"

He pulled his hand free, going back to work. "I saw what my dad leaving did to my mom. I saw that coming for me and Julio, because of my bisexuality, among other reasons, and as much as I cared for him, the thought of being the one left behind, of experiencing even a fraction of what my mom went through, scared the shit out of me."

"So you left him?"

"I did, very publicly, then made a spectacle of myself the

next two weeks. Not my finest moment."

"He said you regretted it."

Bas jerked up the blade. "He said what?"

Jacob's head whipped back at the sharp tone. "He said that you said leaving him was your biggest regret."

"When did he say that?"

"He overheard us, in the tunnel after the race."

"That's why you left?"

Jacob lowered his face again. "I didn't want to make things awkward with the team. And I didn't want to stand in your way. Back to him, if that's what you wanted."

Bas took a final swipe with the clippers and his hand. "One, you belong on the team, including the medley relay squad. You earned that spot and we need you, no matter what happens here between us. And two, what I told Julio was I regretted how I left, not that I did."

"Ah," Jacob sighed. "So he fucked with me after all."

Bas switched off the clippers, set them on the vanity next to his tablet, and pulled the towel off Jacob's shoulders, brushing him off before tossing the cloth in the sink. Bracing his hands on Jacob's knees, Bas lowered himself to kneeling between Jacob's legs. "He fucked with you because I was too much of a coward to tell you how I felt. You're young, smart, perceptive, beautiful. And you get me too—my bisexuality and my reservations. Jacob, you made yourself miserable to give me an out."

"I didn't want to pressure."

"I know, and I don't want to pressure you now. There are going to be so many paths open to you. There's no reason you should stay on mine."

Jacob laid his hands over Bas's, squeezing. There was more of that fire in his voice when he spoke. "And what about the paths for you? You don't think I'm scared too? My mother left us. You could leave me too. My family's not easy, and I'm just a goofball kid who is as far from cool and charming as you can get."

"Don't know if you've realized this, Pup—" Bas lifted a hand, cradling his cheek "—but your uncoolness is the most charming thing about you. You're beautiful, baby." Jacob's lips parted, a whimper escaping. He turned his face into Bas's hand, breath skating over his palm, and Bas's eyes fluttered closed. "If you were mine, I wouldn't let that beauty go. You're everything I want, but I shouldn't stand in your way."

Jacob tangled his fingers with Bas's on his knee and curled his other hand around Bas's neck. "What if I want you to be mine?"

"I'm yours, Pup, if you'll have me."

Jacob's hand around his neck tightened. "Jacob, call me Jacob."

Bas licked his lips and met Jacob's molten mint eyes. It was his turn to make the ask. The same ask Jacob had been brave enough to make multiple times before. It'd be the scariest ask of Bas's life with anyone else, but fear melted away in the face of everything he'd come to know about this remarkable young man. He could trust Jacob with everything. He could make the ask and know his heart was in good hands.

"Stay, Jacob, please."

CHAPTER
SEVENTEEN

BAS BARELY GOT out the *please* before Jacob hurled himself into his lap, sealing their mouths in a hungry kiss and getting as close to Bas as he could.

No doubts, no second-guesses between them, just pure need and want.

Both of them finally on the same page.

He hadn't known what to expect when Bas showed up at the square, then led him back to his room. He'd ignored all the similarities to that night in Vienna—the hand on his back, the gentle words, the careful consideration—because where that night had gone, from lowest to highest to impossibly lower, was not a roller coaster Jacob had wanted to ride again. At best, he'd hoped his team wasn't blistering angry at him for missing the heat.

He hadn't expected to scale an even higher mountain. No, not a mountain, a cliff, because at the top stretched a future he hadn't dared hope for. Bas had laid himself bare, revealing fears Jacob knew all too well. Fears they could tackle together, and Bas wanted that too.

Wanted him to stay. Wanted to stay with him.

Charming uncoolness and all.

He smiled against Bas lips, liking this new view of himself.

Bas fell back on his haunches, and Jacob climbed his body, taking Bas's shirt with him. He growled in frustration when he ran up against their joined mouths. Laughing, Bas pulled back and shucked the shirt.

Jacob started to dive back in, then halted when he saw the two metal pieces hanging in the center of Bas's chest. He'd been so out of it earlier, he hadn't noticed the bullet chain sneaking out from under Bas's collar. His father's dog tags sat right over Bas's sternum, a shiny contrast to his tan skin, Julio's initials to one side, and a blast of colorful tattoos on the other.

Following his gaze, Bas slipped his fingers under the chain, as if to take them off, and Jacob shot out a hand, holding them against Bas's chest. "Don't."

Bas lowered his hands onto Jacob's shoulders. "I didn't want you to be without them, in case you needed them to keep you safe."

"Bas," Jacob choked out.

Bas squeezed his shoulders, and Jacob lifted his eyes, meeting Bas's blazing blue ones. Everything was right there to see. "I want to keep you safe, Jacob. You look after everyone else. Someone has to look after you."

An answer to that soft-spoken question weeks ago in the tattoo parlor. A question that had sounded like a promise then.

But who's looking out for you, Jacob?

Now, the answer sounded like a vow.

"I'd like that," Jacob said, then made a vow of his own. He dragged the hand on Bas's chest, and the tags under it, over to his heart, over the tattoo that was a reminder of fear and regret. "And I'll keep this safe, for you."

Bas's heart thumped beneath his hand, like it'd heard their promises and joined in the agreement. Jacob's heart was beating just as hard, sealing the deal, and Bas was there to catch it. "I'd like that too," he said.

Jacob fell against his body, greedy mouths, heaving chests, and beating hearts slamming together, safety between and around them. Straddling Bas's lap, Jacob rocked their lower bodies together, both of them groaning. Bas trailed fingers down his back, under the waistband of his shorts, holding them flush, while Jacob coasted his hands over Bas's shoulders, neck, and jaw, on the way to Bas's dreads. He pulled them loose, letting them slip through his fingers and around their faces.

Diving deeper into the kiss, he rocked his hips harder against the growing need between them. More certain of himself than he'd been in weeks, Jacob wasn't bashful about asking for what he wanted. He tore his lips away, skating them along Bas's jaw to his ear. "Fuck me, please," he whispered there.

Bas moaned, bucking his hips.

"Is that a yes?" Jacob asked.

Bas's hands traveled up his back, around to frame his face. "Not today," he said, in stark contrast to every signal his body was sending. Only Bas's hands on his face kept it from falling. Bas must have felt the strain. "It's not because I don't want to," he said. He bucked again, ramming his erection against Jacob's. "That's how much I want to."

Jacob thrust his hips in return. "Then why not?"

"Because you have to swim tomorrow." He leaned forward, mouth brushing the shell of Jacob's ear. "And when I fuck you the first time, it's going to be so hard you won't be able to walk, much less swim, for days."

The embarrassing, unintelligible sounds were back. Because "ungh" was all Jacob could manage in response to that promise, his mind and dick otherwise engaged in fantasies of all it entailed.

Just "ungh."

Then Bas went and made it worse. "You're going to fuck me instead."

"Gonna come," he huffed out, Bas's words propelling him to the edge.

"No, baby, and you're not gonna lose your virginity on the bathroom floor either."

"Not helping," Jacob keened.

"Hold tight," Bas said. Arms wrapped around Jacob, he powered up to standing.

The sudden equilibrium shift probably would have gotten the better of Jacob, if he wasn't so busy trying not to come, distracting himself by kissing every inch of Bas's neck as Bas carried him to the bed. His back hit the sun-warmed sheets, then his hips were lifted as Bas stripped him of his shorts and boxers in one go. A rush of cool air blew across his front, but only for a few seconds as Bas finished undressing and carefully laid the dog tags on the table. Naked, Bas stretched out over him, his body settling comfortably atop Jacob's, their cocks grinding together.

Bas kissed over his collarbone and down to tease his nipples, and Jacob lolled his head on the pillow, eyes fluttering, on their way to closed. Until they caught on the shining medals on the table. As much as he wanted to take Bas up on the offer, he shouldn't, not if it'd compromise Bas's race tonight.

He glided his hands over Bas's sides, meaning to get Bas's attention, then losing his train of thought as muscles rippled under his fingertips. He caught it again, though, as a dread brushed his chin, a hint of chlorine in its wake. "You have to swim tonight," he said.

Lifting his head, Bas stared down at him, cheeks flushed, his blue irises obliterated by black pupils. "Which is why I'm going on top." He levered up then, moving his thighs outside of Jacob's, straddling him like Jacob had fantasized half a million times. Jacob ran his hands up and down the powerful muscles while Bas stretched for the drawer, coming back with a condom and lube.

Bas smirked as he ripped the condom open. "Am I going to be able to get this on without you coming?"

"Will you think less of me if I do?"

A hand landed next to Jacob's head, and Bas's lips brushed over his. "I could never think less of you, Jacob."

They sank back into a kiss, getting lost in each other's mouth and the sway of their bodies, until Jacob crept too close to orgasm again. He squeezed Bas thighs. "Now, please, if I've got any shot at this."

Chuckling, Bas slid back and pulled the condom out of the packet. Jacob bit his lip, not giving a damn about his crooked teeth, as Bas rolled the rubber down his cock. That part he survived; it was a closer call when Bas slathered lube all over him, spreading it with long, sure strokes. Then Bas reached his slick hand around behind himself. If Jacob had had any doubts about what Bas was doing, which he didn't, they would have been answered by the slack-jawed look of pleasure that rippled across his face.

And God, was he beautiful, lit by the midday sun streaming into the window. Skin glowing, blond hairs gleaming. Dreads loose, a halo around his face. Tattoos vivid, alive almost. Cock straining, and right there within Jacob's grasp.

He skirted a thumb over the tip, and Bas gasped, jutting his hips forward. Encouraged, Jacob ran his whole hand over the head, collecting the moisture there and stroking down. And back up. Over and over, Bas's hips rocking in time, until groaning, Bas raised up on his knees, took Jacob's cock in hand, and guided it to his ass, slowly lowering himself onto it.

Jacob's grip around Bas's cock faltered as his own pushed past Bas's rim. He dug the nails of his other hand into Bas's thigh, fighting every instinct to thrust up. So warm, so fucking tight. But he had to be careful, let Bas control this part. Better for him too, he told himself. He was looking at a two-thrust max as it was.

The longest ten seconds of his life ended with his cock

fully seated in Bas's ass, clenched tight, so mind-blowingly perfect Jacob wasn't sure which way was up any longer. He arched on the bed, and warm lips came down on one of his nipples, sucking and nipping. Jacob whimpered, finally giving in to the need to thrust.

"Fuck, you feel good," Bas hissed. His hand skated down Jacob's side, and he bowed his back, wedging his cock between them, moisture leaking onto Jacob's torso. Clutching the sheets with one hand, Jacob brought the other between them again, jacking Bas in time with the lift and roll of their hips. "That's it, Jacob. You drive."

Concentrating on the cock in his hand, Jacob stroked and watched Bas's face. Tilted forward, it went slack again, his eyes shuttering, as his chest heaved in time with Jacob's. Like they'd trained, burned into instinct now.

"Not gonna last," Jacob panted after several more thrusts.

Bas expanded in his hand. "Feel me, Jacob. Neither am I. Let's go, together."

He clenched his ass, and Jacob was a goner. Back arched clean off the bed, he tightened his hand around Bas's cock, felt sticky warmth coat his fingers, and he came with a strangled, incomprehensible string of sounds that he wasn't the least bit embarrassed about.

IN THE MIDMORNING light, Bas sat propped against the

headboard, sketching a new design. It had come to him last night, after he'd returned to his room, another gold medal richer, to find the most priceless gift asleep in his bed. He'd taken off his clothes and crawled between the sheets behind Jacob, who'd mumbled, "Congrats," before falling back asleep in his arms.

Still amped from the race, Bas had lain awake for hours, listening to Jacob's light snores, thanking his lucky stars Jacob had given him another chance. There were still things to sort—how this would work with Bas in California, running his shop and swimming, and Jacob in Texas, taking care of his father and finishing school—but Bas was confident they could figure those things out. He and Jacob were growing together, not apart like he and Julio had. That was when the idea had hit him for the new design. He visualized it in his mind, the changes here and there he needed to make, and once satisfied in heart and mind, and his body downshifted from the adrenaline rush, he'd dozed off, lulled to sleep by their matching breaths.

He'd woken with the bells at sunup while Jacob had slept right through them, clearly still exhausted. Bas had slipped out of bed long enough to grab his tablet, then, with Jacob snoring at his side, he'd put stylus to screen, getting the design down. Hours later, just as he put the final touches on the design, Jacob stirred. Squirming on his stomach, he stretched in the larger bed and buried his head in the pillow, hiding from the sun's rays.

Bas smoothed a hand across his shoulders and down his spine. "Morning, Pup."

Jacob turned his head, smiling with his eyes still closed. "You stayed."

Bas's chest ached at the surprise tinging the happiness in Jacob's voice. He never wanted Jacob to doubt him again. He'd gladly stay with him through the night, longer if Jacob would have him. More than that, Bas never wanted to be the source of Jacob's self-doubt again.

Closing the tablet and laying it on the floor, he slinked back under the covers, rolled Jacob onto a hip, and plastered himself to his front, soaking in his warmth. Excited at finding him semihard already.

Good.

Because Bas had a plan to prove to Jacob he had absolutely nothing to doubt, about Bas or himself. Drawing him into a lazy kiss, Bas traced his tongue over Jacob's lips and crooked teeth, worshiping every nook and cranny of Jacob's mouth. Continuing his devotion, he rolled Jacob onto his back and trailed kisses over his collarbone, down his sternum, and around each nipple, before following the trail of dusty blond hair to his erect cock. Swallowing him whole, Bas sucked up and down, making Jacob cry out and bringing him to the brink. Jacob cursed louder as Bas slid off his cock and, with his tongue, paid homage to Jacob's balls, taint and rim, teasing, licking and thrusting the tip of his tongue inside enough to taste and torture. Jacob was back to the edge in no time, a writhing mess begging for release.

Lifting from between Jacob's legs, Bas stretched over him and grasped their hard cocks in his hand, pumping them together. "Yeah, baby, I stayed," he whispered hoarsely against Jacob's lips, so close to coming himself.

Jacob's answering whimper was as good as any fist around Bas's dick.

"Because this—" Bas squeezed them tighter, rutting his cock against Jacob's through his slick grip "—is how much I want you. Always want you, Jacob. Never doubt that."

Jacob snaked out a hand, wove his fingers through Bas's dreads, and hauled him down for a kiss that lasted until come splattered their torsos. Limbs weak, Bas collapsed on top of him, heedless of the mess.

Jacob held him there, legs wrapped around the backs of his thighs and arms tight around his shoulders. "I want more of that," he said, nipping at Bas's neck.

Bas ran a hand down his side, rolling them onto their sides and palming Jacob's ass. "Plenty where that came from." Grinning, he slapped the round, firm cheek, then rolled the rest of the way onto his back and toward the side of the bed. "But we have a race to win first."

Jacob didn't move to follow. "Are you sure?" he asked.

"Am I sure what?"

"That you guys want me to swim with you tonight?"

"Jacob," Bas whispered, dropping another quick kiss on his lips before pulling back and bracing a hand on the bed by his head. "At no point has anyone—me, Alex, Dane, Coach, *anyone*—doubted your ability to swim the medley relay. Fuck, Jacob, don't you realize?" He palmed the side of Jacob's face with his left hand. "You're the one who's held us together."

"I didn't do that," Jacob said, lowering his chin.

Bas gently lifted it. "You made Alex laugh when he was a walking thunder cloud. You didn't single out Dane, when all the rest of us did." Letting go of Jacob's chin, he coasted his hand down, over Jacob's neck and his shoulder to his tattoo, and rubbed a thumb over it. "You gave me a beautiful canvas to work with when I was a nervous wreck over my friend. You let me see you that night, Jacob. And that beauty stuck with me, sunk its claws in deep, and never let go. You're the glue, baby. We need you. And I'm so sorry if I, if we, if anyone ever made you feel like you weren't."

Jacob laid a hand over Bas's, over his tattoo. "I just want to help you guys win. Help you get the gold. I know it means so much, after losing it last time. I was afraid I was fucking that up."

"You didn't fuck up anything." Bas righted himself and offered Jacob a hand. "Will you swim with us tonight? Will you help us win the gold?"

Jacob slipped a hand in his, fingers entwining. "I'll do my best."

Bas lifted Jacob's hand, kissing the back of it. "That's more than enough."

CHAPTER
EIGHTEEN

JACOB BRACED HIS hands on either side of the locker room sink, staring at himself in the vanity mirror. He didn't look much different than he had yesterday. A little less like a Chia Pet, a little more well rested. He and Bas had lazed in bed this morning, until Alex had beat down the door, summoning them for lunch and tape duty. Bas had told Alex to give them five, then they'd taken ten to jerk each other off in the shower before facing the world again.

And the world is what it sounded like inside and outside the locker room tonight. Aside from open water, medley relay was the last swim race at the Games, the main event. All the teams were packed inside the locker room, cheering on their medley relay squads. Outside, the crowd noise was loud enough to rattle the walls. Despite the ruckus, Jacob felt settled, different, even if he didn't look it.

And not just because he'd lost his virginity last night.

After weeks on the bumpiest roller coaster he could have imagined, he'd finally reached the smooth-sailing part. His father looked better every day. He and Bas were together, on the same page, going the same direction. And his team had given him another shot. Between Bas's words yesterday and this morning and watching tape with the guys this afternoon, of their competition and of their own prior practices, Jacob recognized how well they swam and worked together. He believed he was the best breaststroke swimmer for them tonight.

He could help them win.

They would win.

"Burrows."

Jacob shifted his gaze a mirror over, to the reflection of the man who'd tried, and failed, to push him off the rails. "Julio."

"Final race today."

Turning, Jacob folded his arms over his puffed out chest. "And we're going to win it."

"Awfully confident."

"We're the best."

Hip to the adjacent sink, Julio twirled his goggles around his index finger. "Didn't look the best during prelims yesterday."

Jacob wanted to wipe that smirk he'd once thought charming right off the Spaniard's face. "Because I didn't swim, no thanks to you."

"I wanted to be sure you knew what you were getting into, with Bas."

"No, you wanted to be sure I *didn't* get into anything with him. Now, I want to know why."

A familiar rough hand landed on Jacob's left hip and a body he'd come to know intimately fit itself close behind him. "Yeah, explain, J," Bas said.

Julio straightened and squared his shoulders. "I was just trying to save you both from where this is headed."

"You have no idea where it's headed," Bas said.

"I know where we went."

"You want to go back there, don't you?" Jacob said, putting it together. "You started this to fuck with me, and to get revenge against Bas, but 'things changed.'" When Jacob had let on that Bas had already left him, Julio had altered his approach. "You wanted another shot with him, didn't you?"

Julio's gaze drifted over Jacob's shoulder to Bas. "You really think you can make this work? He's still a kid, with two years of school left. And you'd be competing with men and women for his attention. You'd know what you're getting with me."

Bas's arm circled Jacob's waist, tugging him fully back against his chest. "I know what I'm getting with him too. Someone like me. I'm good with that. With him."

"You said you regretted leaving me. We could give it another shot, like Alex and Dane did."

"I said I regretted *how* I left, not that I did. We're not Alex and Dane. They never had a first shot. We did, and it didn't work out."

"And you're going to take a shot on him? You think that'll work out?"

"I am, and I do," Bas said, squeezing him tighter. "Because Jacob's willing to take a shot on me."

Jacob curled a hand over Bas's forearm and glanced over his shoulder, meeting warm blue eyes. "I won't make you sorry."

"I'll try to return the favor."

"Espo," Alex said, joining them. Ever the diplomat, he held out a hand to the other swimmer. "Good luck today." Polite, yet dismissive.

In the face of their united front, Julio surrendered. "Same to you," he said, before heading back to where Team Spain was gathered.

"We're going to beat his ass in the pool today, right?" Alex asked.

"That's the plan," Bas said.

"Pup, you good?" Alex asked.

"I won't let you down."

"Never thought you would." Alex clapped his shoulder. "We're on deck in five." He gave it another pat, then ventured back to their row of lockers, where Dane was leading a chorus of "U-S-A" chants. Jacob turned to join them, but Bas kept him caged in his arms.

"Hey, it's just me here," he said. "You really good?"

"I'm good." Jacob closed the distance between them for a kiss.

Bas pulled back first and leaned their foreheads together. "You know there's no competition, right?"

"In the pool?" Jacob said. "He doesn't stand a chance."

Shaking his head, Bas claimed Jacob's hand and placed it on his chest, right over his heart, like Jacob had done last night. "No, I mean here. You win."

The earlier stolen kiss didn't compare to the one Jacob laid on him then, pouring every bit of his settled, confident feeling into Bas too.

"I believe you," Jacob whispered against his lips. "Now, I'm ready to win the other competition too."

THE FOUR OF them entered the Madrid Aquatic Center together, arms draped over each other's shoulders, the last medley relay team to make their entrance. And an entrance it was. The crowd went wild, shouting and whistling, while the other squads on deck glared. From the press box, cameras flashed at top speed, and neither Alex nor Jacob, on either side of Bas, flinched, their heads held high. And Dane, on the other side of Alex . . . well, Dane did what Dane did best and smiled even wider.

Bas smiled wider too. This was it. For all the marbles. And for Bas and Alex and Dane, at twenty-six, it could be their last Olympic event, ever. Barring injury, Jacob would be back in four years, and Bas would happily cheer him on from the stands. But right here, right now, Bas soaked in the thrill of competition and reveled in the fact he was playing at the highest level of the sport he loved.

With the three best men he knew. His squad. His brothers and his lover.

They gathered behind lane three, ignoring, as best they could, the dark looks from Julio's Spanish squad a lane over.

Coach stepped in between them, cutting off the rivals teams' view. "Huddle up."

They closed their circle, heads together, Coach standing between Jacob and Dane. "Anything else I need to say here?" His dark eyes bounced to each of them.

"No, Coach," Alex said.

"Go time," Bas added.

"Gold time." Dane grinned.

"Pup?" Alex said, eyeing Jacob across the circle.

Jacob squinted one eye, hitched one side of his mouth, and in full pirate accent said, "Aye, Aye, Captain."

Their chants of "U-S-A" in the huddle matched the chants of their fans, including the rest of the men's and women's teams in the stands. The roar only grew louder with team introductions. And louder still—deafening—when, as Team USA was introduced, Alex pulled Dane in for a back-bending kiss. Camera's clicked, catcalls were shouted, and Alex smiled against Dane's lips bigger than Bas had ever seen. His best friend wasn't one for flash and show—that was Dane's specialty—but Bas figured he was making a statement, an exclamation point on the signed papers Bas's mother had sent over. Alex was happy, proud, and for once, enjoying himself. Bas was one hundred percent behind it, waving his arms and amping up the crowd.

Because if Alex was this confident, this loose, they were going to win. He had no doubt. Jacob knew it too, smiling at him with eyes so bright Bas considered putting on a similar display. But that wasn't them. Not yet, at least. What was them was Bas yanking the pup into a headlock and knuckling his head.

"No competition," he whispered in Jacob's ear, dropping

a kiss there that no one would see with his dreads down. Jacob slipped the hold, laughing.

As intros finished, Bas tied up his dreads, wrangled them into his cap, and strapped his goggles on, resting them over his brow. When the bell rang for swimmers to get in the water, Bas stepped to the side of the pool with Alex. Most swimmers jumped in themselves. But dating back to their days at SC, Bas always gave Alex a hand down into the pool. It was their routine—solidarity and friendship, no matter the situation.

"Proud of you," Bas said, holding the hand clasp.

Alex curled his hand tighter. "Proud of you too."

"You remember your promise?" Bas said.

"We win gold, I finally get a tattoo."

"Holding you to that."

Alex nodded. "Do your part, and I'll be there."

"Count on it." Bas released Alex's hand and stepped back, slapping the deck to rile up the crowd some more.

It was so loud in the arena, the "Swimmers, take your mark" announcement was nearly drowned out.

Alex grabbed the bar at the bottom of the block, braced his feet against the wall, and hauled himself up into starting position. Dane leaned over, slapping the block. "Smoke 'em, babe."

The horn blew, Alex arched off the wall, and did just that. Swimming at world-record speed when he tapped the far wall, it seemed barely a blink before he was halfway down the return lap.

"All yours, Pup," Bas said, with a tap to Jacob's ass that,

if anyone cared to look, lingered a little too long.

Jacob smiled over his shoulder as he lined up on the block, beautiful body coiled, ready to launch.

Alex's fingers slammed the wall beneath the block, and Jacob was off, the exchange perfect. He was just as beautiful in the water as he was out of it. Missing the heat yesterday hadn't dulled him in the slightest. If anything, he was swimming with more power and speed. He was earning it, his spot, even if no one asked him to, proving it to himself as much as anyone. And maybe also proving it to Julio, who Jacob left in the dust at the turn, setting a blistering return pace.

Bas stepped up on the block, getting into position, eyes locked through his goggles on Jacob. Each time his lover breached the water's surface to breathe, Bas inhaled with him. Breathing together like they'd trained. Like they had in the alley in Vienna, like they had in bed together yesterday, like they had in the shower this morning.

In time, *here*, together.

Bas didn't have to think about the exchange. It was timed to perfection.

He hit the water clean and came up arms wheeling, legs kicking, breath still in sequence with the pace Jacob had set. And for the first time in four years, Bas swam without weight. No worry, no regret, no fear. Just pure instinct driving him. Happiness, for himself and Jacob, for Alex and Dane, pushed him faster. He touched the far wall, turned, kicked, and looked under the water to either side. Nothing. He was smiling as he came back out of the water, eyes dead ahead, locked on Jacob, who was pounding the deck next to Dane getting ready on the block.

Those fiery mint dimes brought Bas the rest of the way home, his fingers crashing into the wall as Dane sailed overhead.

Big Red full-throttle was a sight to behold. The fastest swimmer in the world, swimming like he had nothing and everything to lose. Bas couldn't tear his eyes away as Jacob and Alex hauled him out of the pool. Hanging over their shoulders, he gulped for breath and watched the master at work. Dane's turn was a full half second ahead of everyone else and well under Olympic and World record pace.

Alex slid out from under Bas's arm, going to the edge of the pool and putting himself right in Dane's line of sight. Impossibly, Dane swam faster. Like he hit another gear no one knew he had. Bas held Jacob tighter, remembering that feeling from seconds ago. The need to get home.

Dane was at the wall in a blink, torso breaking the water, gasping for air and ripping off his cap and goggles. Alex was half in the water, arms looped over his neck, pointing at the clock. The time registered, and Bas punched the air with his raised fist.

Gold.

With Olympic and world records.

And with Jacob by his side, staring up at him, victorious and happy.

Beautiful.

CHAPTER
NINETEEN

BAS'S TATTOO PARLOR had never been so packed. Nor so festive.

Alex and Dane had moved out from Colorado the day after Christmas and spent the past week ignoring the moving boxes in their new place by stringing all manner of New Year's decorations around Bas's. Both in the shop and in his apartment upstairs.

"Gotta make a good impression for the pup," Dane had said, grinning as he and Alex bustled around. A giant red-headed elf hanging gold and silver streamers and tinsel, while his dark-haired Santa washed the sheets and left lube and a Costco-sized box of condoms on the freshly made bed.

Not that Bas didn't appreciate it. He had plans to put the bed and condoms to good use. It'd been October since he'd seen his boyfriend—a trip out to Texas for Jacob's birthday—and no amount of Skype or FaceTime calls since could make up for the real thing.

And it was real.

Bas believed that now, about Alex and Dane, and about him and Jacob. Five months ago, he'd been running as fast as he could away from Jacob, trying to protect them both, and now all he wanted to do was run to him, the safest place for both of them. He wanted Jacob in his arms again, under him, writhing. So what the fuck had made him think it was a good idea to invite the whole team here and delay their reunion?

Oh right, he hadn't thought that. Dane had, and as was his way since that night he'd come out to the team, he'd rallied everyone behind him. A New Year's party for the squad, a housewarming for him and Alex, and a chance for Bas to ink their team tattoos. Even Mo was flying out, through Vegas, where he'd connected on the same flight with Jacob. They'd sent Bas a selfie from the plane—Mo ruffling the curls his boyfriend had grown back, at Bas's urging. Bas couldn't wait to weave his fingers through the dirty-blond tangles, draw Jacob's face in close, taste his—

"Mind out of the gutter, Stewart."

Bas looked up from the table of supplies he was preparing and glared at his best friend. "I'm wishing evil thoughts on your boy right now."

Alex leaned against the chair, hands splayed. "You could have said no."

Bas's gaze skated over Alex's shoulder, to Kevin and Mike pulling bottles of champagne out of the fridge, to Leah, Sean, and Natalie standing nearby chatting, to their other teammates wandering around, talking and admiring the tattoo designs that covered the shop walls. They weren't all getting inked tonight, that'd be too much work, but they'd be in town for the week, dropping in and hanging out, celebrating their victories. And tonight, on New Year's Eve, celebrating the end of one year and the start of the next.

No, he couldn't have said no. Bas wouldn't have wanted to pass this up. Or the chance to hold Alex to his promise. Bas accepting Dane's party idea was as much about peer pressure as anything.

"You really going to let me ink you?" Bas said.

"We made a deal, didn't we? We won the gold." Alex crossed his arms, fingers digging into his biceps. Yes, they'd made a deal, but obviously Alex still didn't like the idea. Terrified of needles, he'd avoided the tattoo tradition through college and the last Olympics.

"We did make a deal," Bas said. "But I know this—" he lifted the tattoo machine "—is not your idea of fun."

Alex shook his head. "We've won, in the pool and out of it." Smiling, he glanced over his shoulder at Dane, who was at the center of the melee up front. "We've all conquered fears this year," he said, turning his dark eyes back to Bas. "Think it's time I conquered my last one too."

Bas walked around the end of the chair and yanked his best friend into a hug. "All right, then. You wanna go first? Get it over with?"

Alex paled but nodded. "Think that's probably best."

"You are the captain." Bas grabbed the tattoo machine and slapped Alex's shoulder. The sound was echoed up front by the pop of champagne corks.

"What are you fools doing?" Alex shouted, sounding exactly like Coach. "You're not supposed to do that until everyone is here."

Sean lifted his arm, the one not curled around Natalie, and pointed at the door. "Everyone *is* here."

Bas had missed the jingle of the doorbell, its tinkling muffled by the crowd noise. Teammates parting, Bas saw Dane and his mentor, Mo, clenched in a hug. The door closed and out from behind them stepped Jacob.

Motionless by the chair, Bas swept his eyes over his boyfriend. Dressed in jeans, a hoodie, and the *I am the Real Dread Pirate Roberts* T-shirt Bas had given him for his birthday, Jacob looked beautiful and rested, not strung out like he had been in October, juggling Bas's visit with midterms. Things were good at home with his family too, Bas knew, from their nightly calls.

Eyes trained on Bas, Jacob smiled big, flashing his adorably crooked front teeth. Standing there, his face lit with the twinkling Christmas lights Dane had strung and the flashing neon *Tattoo* sign in the front window, Jacob looked at home.

In Bas's home.

This was the start of *their* story.

Alex slipped the tattoo machine from his hand and slapped his ass. "Go."

Bas made it two steps before Jacob dropped his bags and lunged, slamming into him and going right for a kiss. Bas ignored the whistles and catcalls of his teammates, enthusiastically returning his boyfriend's greeting.

"I missed you," Jacob mumbled against his lips.

"I missed you too." Parting, Bas framed Jacob's beautiful face in his hands, thumbs brushing over scruffy cheeks. "It's good seeing you here."

"It's good to be here."

More champagne corks popped. "Let's get this party started," Dane declared.

The team cheered in agreement, and Jacob dropped another quick kiss on Bas's lips. "Work fast," he said, eyes heating.

"You got it." Bas turned and took the machine back from a grinning Alex. "Cap's up first."

PARTY WINDING DOWN, Jacob snuck into the dressing room at the rear of Bas's shop. Back turned to the mirror, he untaped the bandage and admired the new ink on his right delt. The same style as his other tattoo, this one—a red, white, and blue war eagle with Olympic rings stretched between its wings—was an ode to their captain's Mexican-American heritage and also to the war they'd waged to finally get the gold. It was meaningful and perfect, something he could show others with pride, just like his Longhorn tattoo. Josh had been right. The ink had drastically increased Jacob's coolness factor this past semester. Or maybe that had more to do with his three Olympic medals. Or his gorgeous boyfriend who'd shown up midsemester and whisked Jacob away to his hotel room between exams.

Just thinking about that week—a whirlwind of torturous midterms, Bas making sure he ate and slept, and then, when his tests were over, torture of a different, much better, sort—

made Jacob's already hard problem even harder.

Jacob wanted that again, the glasses of champagne he'd guzzled before straddling the tattoo chair only adding fuel to the fire. But he didn't want to pressure Bas, who'd worked for hours on the first round of team tattoos. Instead of worrying about where his dick was going to go, Jacob should be massaging the broad shoulders that had started to slump under the ink-stained T-shirt, or helping pull up the dreads that had come loose from Bas's topknot, or making a run to In-N-Out for food.

He glanced down at his tented jeans. Er, maybe not yet.

"All right, all right." Dane's extra-long, champagne-slurred drawl echoed from the front of the shop, as did the answering laughs. "Let's get out of here and leave the lovebirds to it. Brunch at our place in the morning."

"I can't promise it's unpacked," Alex added.

According to Bas, it wasn't unpacked at all, except the kitchen. For Dane's home cooking, Jacob would gladly eat off boxes. Hell, he'd even help unpack a few.

"Anyone need me to write down the address?" Alex said.

"You emailed it to us, Cap," Sean replied, as the bell over the front door jingled, again and again, the team filing out.

"Night, Pup," Dane hollered.

Jacob poked his head and arm out from between the dressing room curtains, waving. "See you tomorrow."

He slipped back into the dressing room, fixed the bandage on his delt, and unbuttoned his jeans, attempting to fix something else. Only to have the curtain wrenched open midadjustment. Jacob's eyes darted up and met Bas's in the mirror, just as they had that night five months ago. Different mirror, different color on the walls and curtains, but Bas's eyes were the same blazing blue as they had been then.

"Problem?" he asked.

Jacob's confidence, between then and now, was also radically different. He still blushed, no help for that, but he made no bones about his invitation. "Not uncommon, I understand. Want to help me solve it?"

Bas accepted the invite, closing the distance between them and laying a hand on his back. "Pull it out," he rumbled in Jacob's ear.

Pushing his jeans and boxers down, waistbands half over his ass, Jacob reached his other hand in and freed his cock, stroking himself and letting his boyfriend see what he'd done to him.

Bas reached a hand around, covering Jacob's and stroking him together. "You were so fucking beautiful that night." His other hand caressed the dimples in his back, then drifted down, teasing his crack. "Tonight too."

Jacob rested his head on Bas's shoulder and kissed the underside of his jaw. "When you caught me that night, I was imagining this." He thrust into their grip, moisture coating their fingers and slicking the strokes.

Bending his head, Bas licked and nibbled at the crook of his neck. "How's the real thing compare?"

"Better." But there was something better still. Moving a hand behind him, he palmed Bas's cock through his jeans, gliding up and down the hard length. "It'd be even better if you fucked me."

Groaning, Bas dragged his open mouth up Jacob's neck, to his mouth, before he rotated Jacob and dove into a kiss that left Jacob weak, only Bas's arms around him holding him up. When Bas stepped back to drop his pants and boxer-briefs and roll on a condom, Jacob slouched against the wall and enjoyed the view, so much better in person than on Skype. Until Bas tossed his shirt and Jacob's attention was drawn to the bandage over his left pec.

"Your team tattoo?" he ventured. Bas usually reserved his arms, shoulders, and back for those, the only ink on the left side of his chest the *JE* tattoo Jacob had made peace with. But maybe this summer had changed that.

Bas shook his head. "I'll get one of my staff to do the team tat."

"Then what's—"

His words died as Bas removed the bandage, exposing the tattoo underneath. If Jacob thought his head was spinning before, it was a tilt-a-whirl now. He wasn't sure his legs would hold him, but he had to get a closer look, touch what his eyes could hardly believe. He reached out a shaking hand, and gently traced the lines of the familiar design, still a little pink around the edges. He must have had it done a couple of weeks ago.

Hand to his cheek, Bas brushed a kiss against his temple. "It's okay, Pup?"

At a loss for words, Jacob nodded, eyes blurring as they drifted again to the *J* and *B* stenciled into the snout of the Longhorn tattoo, an otherwise perfect match to his own. Right over where the previous two letters had been inked.

Over Bas's heart.

A breathy "Bas" was all Jacob could manage.

"I know you're young," Bas said, caressing his cheek. "And this, us, is young. We don't know where it'll lead." He lowered his hand, covering Jacob's where it rested just to the side of the new tattoo. "But I want you here. I love you, Jacob."

They'd never said the words. Jacob had felt them—in Madrid over the summer, in Texas this past fall, in his own heart and in Bas's kisses, and in the way Bas made love to him—but Jacob had held back from saying them, still cautious of asking too much, from Bas and himself. They had committed to giving this thing between them a shot. To stay. With Bas's words now, and with the manifestation of that love inked on his skin, Jacob, filled with confidence, decided to risk asking for more.

"I have enough credits to graduate early, at the end of this summer. I talked to Dane, and with my CompSci degree, I'm going to come work for him, at his new programming company."

"Come work for him?"

"Here, in LA." Jacob glanced up from the tattoo, meeting Bas's wide eyes. "If that's okay with you?"

"But what about Davis? I can't take you away from him if he needs you."

Bas and Davis had clicked from first meeting, his dad confessing he'd known there was more between them as far back as Madrid, having noticed his dog tags around Bas's neck that day on the phone. Now, Bas asked about his dad on every call, understanding how important he was to Jacob. It meant the world to Jacob that Bas would sacrifice his own happiness for Jacob's father's. He—*they*—didn't have to, though.

"My father has PTSD," Jacob said. "He's doing well, not a single flashback the past six months. And he has a new fiancée, who also happens to be a nurse."

"He and Darlene made it official?"

Jacob nodded, smiling. "'Didn't want to waste any more time,' he said. And Josh's parents are right across the street too. My dad's in good hands."

Bas lifted his own, framing Jacob's face. "Will you be? Are you sure?"

Angling his face, Jacob kissed first one, then the other of Bas's palms, loving how Bas always held him so gently, so safely. He craved that strong, gentle hold every day. "I may be young," he said, "but I love you, Sebastian, and I want to be with you, here. Can I stay?"

Arms wrapping around him, one hand cradling his head, the other protecting the tender spot on his shoulder, Bas pushed him back against the wall and kissed him long and deep. Jacob groaned into his mouth, lifting a leg over his hip and grinding their cocks together. Bas slid a hand around, teasing open Jacob's hole, readying him. Several minutes and two fingers later, Jacob ripped his mouth away, head falling back in Bas's hand. "Is that a yes?"

Bas righted his face, pressing their foreheads together. "Fuck yes, I want you here. Move in with me."

He dove for another kiss, and Jacob dodged. "On one

condition." Bas lifted a brow, and Jacob lowered his hand over Bas's heart and the new tattoo. "Add your initials to mine too. Mark me. Claim what's yours."

Growling, Bas hauled him up, then slowly slid inside him, controlling Jacob's descent so the pressure wouldn't burn too much. Always looking out for him, always keeping him safe.

Jacob wound his arms around Bas's neck, gaining leverage to pull himself up and drop back down, riding Bas's cock. "Will you do that for me?" He loosened Bas's dreads, and they fell around them, creating the cocoon Jacob loved so much.

Bas kissed him rough, thrusting up and hitting that spot inside of Jacob. "Yeah, I'll mark you." He kissed him deeper, thrusting faster, neither of them able to hold out long for this first reunion. "I'll claim you." Wrapping a hand around Jacob's cock, he stroked him right to the edge, hips pumping in time. "Just like you've claimed me. I love you, Jacob."

"Love you too," tumbled from Jacob's lips as he came.

ACKNOWLEDGMENTS

This book was hard, y'all, in part because I challenged myself to step outside my usual suspense shoes (only one hacking scene!) and in part because it's so personal. But for all the hair pulling, cursing, coffee, and self-doubt that went into *Medley*, I'm very happy with how Bas and Jacob's love story turned out. Special thanks to my agent, Laura Bradford, for her enthusiasm for this project, to Kristi for the editorial assistance, to Garrett and LC for the cover and layout, to Tera, Mirna and Anna for their beta reads, to my author support crew who worked overtime holding my hand with this one, and to Judith and Keyanna for making my hectic life a little less so. I owe you all a big, Dane-style Southern breakfast to show my appreciation. And finally, thank you, readers, for embracing Alex, Dane, Bas, and Jacob as they swam their way to love and gold. I hope you enjoyed the race with us!

ALSO BY
LAYLA REYNE

Changing Lanes series
Relay

Agents Irish and Whiskey series
Single Malt
Cask Strength
Barrel Proof
Tequila Sunrise

ABOUT
THE AUTHOR

Author Layla Reyne was raised in North Carolina and now calls San Francisco home. She enjoys weaving her bi-coastal experiences into her stories, along with adrenaline-fueled suspense and heart pounding romance. When she's not writing stories to excite her readers, she downloads too many books, watches too much television, and cooks too much food with her scientist husband, much to the delight of their smushed-face, leftover-loving dogs. Layla is a member of Romance Writers of America and its Kiss of Death and Rainbow Romance Writers chapters. She was a 2016 RWA® Golden Heart® Finalist in Romantic Suspense.

You can find Layla at laylareyne.com, on Twitter, Facebook, Instagram and Pinterest as @laylareyne, and in her reader group on Facebook—Layla's Lushes.

CPSIA information can be obtained
at www.ICGtesting.com
Printed in the USA
LVHW031538060619
620404LV00035B/487